Murd

on

Christmas

Eve 🎄

A Dodo Dorchester Mystery

Book 6

by

ANN SUTTON

Published by

Wild Poppy Publishing LLC
Highland, UT 84003

Distributed by Wild Poppy Publishing

Cover design by Julie Matern
Cover Design ©2021 Wild Poppy Publishing LLC

Edited by Jolene Perry

Dedicated to
Matthew Matern

Style Note

I am a naturalized American citizen born and raised in the United Kingdom. I have readers in America, the UK, Australia, Canada and beyond. But my book is set in the United Kingdom.

So which version of English should I choose?

I chose American English as it is my biggest audience, my family learns this English and my editor suggested it was the most logical.

This leads to criticism from those in other English-speaking countries, but I have neither the time nor the resources to do a special edition for each country.

I do use British words, phrases and idioms whenever I can (unless my editor does not understand them and then it behooves me to change it so that it is not confusing to my readers).

Table of Contents

Dodo peered out the low-slung, passenger window of Rupert's little green and black Hudson Roadster to get a first glimpse of *Knightsbrooke Priory* in the winter twilight, a mixture of excitement and nerves dueling in her chest. She rested her forehead on the cool glass, her eyes fixing on the light of the full moon.

Rupert had invited her to spend Christmas with his family after he and her lady's maid, Lizzie, rescued her from being kidnapped in her last case. A case she thought might be her last. A crazed drug dealer had threatened to kill her, and it had rattled her more than she cared to admit. Escaping to *Knightsbrooke Priory*, ancestral home of the Danforths, was the ideal way to put some distance in time and space between herself and the trauma. She would tell her family eventually…but not yet.

"It was a castle first, built in the mid-thirteenth century," said Rupert, bringing her back to the present. "A veritable fortress with soldiers and everything. Hence, the fact that the front looks like a fort, there aren't many windows and the name '*knight*'. Then it was left to rack and ruin until the church commandeered it for a Catholic monastery at the beginning of the fourteenth century. Which explains the name '*priory*'." Every word was laced with pride. "After the Reformation it lay empty but for rooks, when an enterprising ancestor bought it for a song and bankrupted himself trying to restore it."

As he spoke, the dark, foreboding castle rose from the frosty ground like an austere, warty maiden aunt.

Dodo shrank back. "Golly, our place is practically new compared to this. It was built in the early nineteenth century."

Rupert reached for her hand. "I can assure you that it has been modernized inside but it does get rather cold in the winter."

Dodo drew her soft, white, fur coat tighter.

As they neared the front entrance of the fortified manor house, its sharp portcullis of iron, and traditional fort stonework came into focus. High curtain walls flanked the ancient gates and towers punctuated the blank façade. Dodo could see small openings in the stone walls where soldiers had once defended the place with arrows. The impression was forbidding and somber.

A long, straight driveway edged by an avenue of small trees led to the front, and the car bounced and bumped over the irregular, pot-holed driveway.

Coming to a stop in front, the threatening portcullis was raised, and several shadowy servants spilled out. Rupert walked around the car and opened the door for Dodo. The recent shared ordeal had moved their relationship to another level, and she took comfort in his firm hand. Meeting his family was a big step.

Dodo looked into the dark sky as a brisk wind kicked up, dragging the clouds across the stars like a curtain and plunging the front of the castle into even greater darkness.

Taking a deep breath, Dodo grabbed Rupert's hand as they crunched across the gravel, under the iron grating, and through an ancient, scarred front door into a vast, tomb-like entryway with an impossibly high ceiling and rustic chandelier.

Her breath created soft, white plumes in the air.

At the back of the stone foyer, stood a tall, pungent, evergreen, festooned with friendly, glittering garlands and small electric lights that was at odds with the atmosphere.

Dodo reluctantly relinquished her coat to a maid as a couple of energetic Labradors bounded to greet them, followed by a tall, lanky girl of about seventeen. She was undoubtedly Rupert's younger sister, Julia.

"Rupie!" cried the girl, flinging her arms around Rupert's neck and jumping into his arms as the dogs pressed against their legs, tongues lolling. Her light brown hair bounced as Rupert swung the cheerful girl around with ease, kissing her cheek before setting her back on the ground.

"Rupie?" mouthed Dodo with a wicked grin. He shrugged and grabbed Dodo's hand. "Julia, meet Dorothea."

"Dodo, please!" protested Dodo.

Julia placed both hands to her mouth and squealed. "Oh!" she cried. "I've been counting the minutes till you got here. I follow your career in the fashion industry whenever I can." She looked down at her rather plain dress. "I'm hoping you can give me some advice. Mummy knows nothing about that kind of thing." She was as eager as the puppies panting by her feet.

"Of course. I'd love nothing more," Dodo replied truthfully. If her calling in life was to change the world one bad wardrobe at a time, she welcomed the challenge.

Julia grabbed Dodo's hand. "Come on. Everyone's in the drawing room." She dragged the pair forward with her long, gangly arms and pushed open a heavy arched door, the dogs slipping through their legs.

This room was in stark contrast to the gloomy entry. Here it was bright and warm, bursting with boughs of holly and pine. A friendly fire roared in the most enormous fireplace Dodo had ever seen and comfortable maroon sofas made a square around the giant hearth. Heavy, velvet curtains covered the windows helping the large room feel cozy and intimate.

An extremely tall, big-boned woman of about fifty, rose from one of the settees, her arms outstretched. Whatever Dodo had imagined Henrietta Danforth to be, she was not it. Dodo could see little of her son in the broad, lined face.

"Dorothea," she said in a voice as warm and comforting as hot cocoa. "We are so happy to have you here at *Knightsbrooke Priory.*"

"Thank you, and please, call me Dodo."

Rupert's father came to stand beside his wife. Slightly shorter than her, he was a good four inches shy of his son. In his face she recognized Rupert, but unlike his son, his head was shiny as a new penny. "Dashed happy to meet you!" he bellowed with a voice that resonated with military precision. He took Dodo's hand and kissed it. "About time Rupert brought someone home with more than an ounce of intelligence."

Dodo tapped her nose. "I wouldn't rush to judgement so soon, Mr. Danforth." She delivered her patented smile and was happy to see his eyes widen as he laughed. "Oh, jolly good!" He chuckled. "Jolly good! But please, call me Rupert."

3

Dodo glanced at Rupert. "That's why they call me Rupie."

Dodo raised her brows, biting back a grin.

"Please sit," said Mrs. Danforth as she showed Dodo to the seat she had recently vacated. "And call me Etta – everyone else does." Everything about her was oversized, her nose, her lips, her hands.

When Dodo was settled, Mrs. Danforth pointed to a slight, elderly woman on the sofa straight across. "Here is Rupert's grandmother, Adelaide Danforth."

A frail looking woman with fight in her ice blue eyes nodded with a genuine smile. "How lovely to meet you," she said in a voice as fragile as her frame. "Julia has been telling us all about you."

Rupert's mother pointed to another person hidden in the sofa perpendicular to Dodo's. "I believe you already know Beatrice?"

"Hello, Dodo."

The last time Dodo had seen Beatrice, she was on her way to a convalescent home, suffering withdrawals from opium. Though still clearly recovering, her metamorphosis was astonishing. The sallow, gray skin had transformed to a healthy peach and the once foggy eyes were now alight with excitement and intelligence. They had met in London when Beatrice was accused of murder and Dodo had worked to uncover the true killer.

She looked nothing like her mother.

"Beatrice!" Dodo leapt up to embrace her friend, then moved to allow Rupert to do the same. Unashamed to show his emotions, he gathered Beatrice into his arms as she buried her face in his neck. Dodo's heart squeezed and she pretended not to notice Mrs. Danforth wiping her eye.

"Now, tell me all about yourself," Rupert's mother said to Dodo, shoving a handkerchief up the sleeve of a sturdy, gray cardigan that covered her shapeless dress.

Dodo told them about her family and her work with the French fashion house of Dubois and various British designers.

"I think you have missed an important part of your story," said Rupert, his eyes twinkling.

"Ah, your son is referring to my detective work."

4

"Detective work?" gasped Etta Danforth, her formerly friendly face taking a dramatic downturn. Rupert had not told his parents about the murder Beatrice had been implicated in, for obvious reasons.

Seeing the alarm in Etta's face, Dodo opted for lighthearted. "Though it pains me to say it, murder does seem to follow me like bees to honey."

Mrs. Danforth's laugh was more like an expression of anxiety. "Let's hope that doesn't ring true over Christmas," she said, her droopy eyes telegraphing a hint of concern.

"Dodo has worked with Scotland Yard on more than one occasion," Rupert chimed in, steering the conversation away from the spark of fear. "But we met during a case where the police could not even reach us. She solved that one all by herself."

"Not alone," she contradicted him. "Lizzie, my maid, and Rupert were invaluable assistants." She looked around the room to find that all eyes were on her.

"You were involved in a murder?" growled Mr. Danforth. "You didn't mention it, son."

The palpable change of atmosphere in the room was confusing.

Am I missing something?

It *was* unusual for a young society woman to be involved in anything as vulgar as murder, but the Danforth family's reaction suggested that their disapproval stemmed from something more fundamental.

"I thought I would wait until Dodo was here since she deserves all the credit, Pops."

Dodo saw a nervous glance pass between his parents, and she could feel the initial goodwill, slipping away. Minds needed changing. A gifted storyteller, she prepared to deliver her account in a way that regaled and persuaded her doubtful audience.

By unspoken agreement that she would not relate the most recent case involving his sister, Rupert ceded Dodo the stage. She artfully spun the tale of the murder where she and Rupert had met, on the Devonshire moors.

5

Her delivery seemed to work its magic on Mr. Danforth and the other family members, but his mother was another story. Instead of relaxing, Etta Danforth seemed even more tense and withdrawn.

"An illegitimate son who was taking his revenge, you say," said Mr. Danforth. "Whatever next?"

"How clever of you to solve such a tricky crime," announced Adelaide Danforth, almost licking her lips. "And all while you were trapped together in the fog. How romantic."

"I think it's terribly exciting," gushed Julia, eyes bright as crystals.

The butler entered the room and announced dinner.

Dodo looked down at her traveling clothes, a gray wool skirt and practical jumper. "But we haven't changed," whispered Dodo into Rupert's ear.

"Don't worry. My parents understand that we have just arrived. You can stun everyone tomorrow." His nose tickled her cheek sending a delightful wave of pleasure through her, offsetting the nagging concern that his mother disapproved.

The dining room was vast, obviously built for a full garrison, and she missed her fur coat. Someone had tried to personalize it at some point, but its dimensions did not lend itself to intimate conversation with the other diners. The grand table had been built in proportion to the room with chairs heavy enough to form an effective blockade if needed. There were plenty of electric lights and candles, but the lack of large windows and the impossibly dark wood absorbed most of the light making the room feel heavy.

The seven of them were mostly spread out around the perimeter of the table, but someone had arranged for her seat to be right next to Rupert. His diminutive grandmother was all but swallowed by her chair, like a tiny pearl in its oyster bed, but her eyes were shrewd and bright, and Dodo could see that she was being sized up by a pro. There was obviously more to the tiny woman than met the eye.

As the soup was served, Rupert's father filled them in on the agenda.

6

"Lady Millicent Marlborough, mother of the current Duke of Swithers, will be joining us tomorrow. She's an old friend of my mother." He nodded in Adelaide's direction with his polished head.

"We were great friends in our youth," said Adelaide in her warbled voice. "Thick as thieves until my marriage when I moved. Haven't seen her in years, but she has come to settle matters with a solicitor in the area and I was eager to see her. Who knows how many more Christmases we will see?"

"Quite so, quite so," agreed Mr. Danforth. "Then my sister, Ruby, and her husband, Lawrence Quintrell, will join us."

"Don't forget the vicar, Daddy," said Julia with more than a little enthusiasm.

"Ah, yes. The vicar." He ran a hand over his bald pate. "He's new to the living and unmarried. Want to make a good impression on him for his first Christmas in Knightsbrooke."

Adelaide's mouth hitched at the corner. "A fine-looking young cleric who has not gone unnoticed around here. We'll be a lively party with all the young people," she said, a diamond comb winking from her white hair.

Etta frowned.

"Julia has planned some festive activities—" began her father.

"Oh yes!" Julia interrupted. "We're going to hook up one of the horses to the old sleigh and go tobogganing on Knights Hill."

"I hope I am not to be included in this?" croaked Adelaide with a wry smile spreading across her cracked lips.

"Oh no, Granny! You silly thing. Not even Mummy and Daddy are coming. It's just for us young ones." She waved her serviette at the absurdity of her aged grandmother flying down the hill on a toboggan. "Then we will make snowmen, and when we are so cold we cannot stand it anymore, we will come home for some hot Whipcoll. It will be so much fun!"

"It's a good thing I ordered some extra brandy then," Mr. Danforth said, unexpectedly tipping his bowl to get the last of the soup.

"The others will all be arriving tomorrow, on Christmas Eve," explained Etta.

7

"Will we play sardines?" asked Rupert. "It is a Christmas tradition after all."

"Oh yes!" agreed Julia. "We'll play that on Christmas day after all the presents have been opened, and after dinner we will play charades, like usual."

Dodo cast a glance at Beatrice who had shown very little appetite when they had been together in London but who was tucking into her meal now. The shadows under her eyes were almost gone. Beatrice flicked a thick-lashed glance up at Dodo and smiled. She exhibited a natural, country prettiness that had been all but disguised by her addiction. Dodo felt like she was meeting her for the first time.

The footmen removed the soup plates and replaced them with robust china plates as they offered steaming ham and lightly roasted potatoes. Dodo idly wondered if the kitchens were as primitive as the rest of the house appeared to suggest.

After dinner, Dodo slipped the button undone on her skirt waistband and they all retired back to the cozy drawing room for coffee, including Mr. Danforth. He settled his mother close to the fire as her head bobbed in sleep, and they all chattered comfortably, except Etta who was quiet and tense.

About twenty minutes later, when all the coffee cups were empty, Adelaide appeared to stir.

"Changed my will... Poopsie," she muttered as she shifted her position.

Dodo tilted her head in interest, catching Rupert's eye.

"One thing you need to know about Granny," Rupert whispered into her ear. "She is always threatening to change her will. I'm sure her solicitor dreads her phone calls." He laughed quietly. "The thing is, she's absolutely loaded. Father inherited the estate, of course, but Granny's family settled everything on her. She is fantastically wealthy."

Dodo looked over at the petite figure whose head leaned against the side of the deep sofa. In sleep she looked younger as the deep wrinkles relaxed.

"Does your family worry when she changes her will?" she asked.

Rupert wrinkled his straight nose. "It's all hot air. She calls the solicitor regularly but rarely does anything other than small alterations. But who knows, Granny is certainly not your traditional grandmother, and she may delight in surprising us after her passing." He traced patterns in Dodo's palm as he spoke. "But we don't give it too much attention since she's not going anywhere. She's strong as an ox and will likely outlive us all."

Chapter 2

Christmas Eve dawned bright and frigid.

As Dodo peeked through the frost patterned windows of her vast but comfortable bedroom, a fresh layer of white snow greeted her, sparkling like diamonds in the sunlight. A childish excitement bubbled inside. The contrast with the impossibly blue sky could not have been more perfect.

She clasped her hands under her chin. *A white Christmas!*

"I've looked out your woolens and some cotton undergarments—silk won't cut it today," said Lizzie who had arrived by train a day before Dodo, and was already settled into the servant's quarters. "I've got mine on. It's pretty cold in this place. How old *is* it?"

"Older than dirt, my dear." Dodo pulled her mouth down. "Certain rooms are comfy, but I fear the others are like an ice cave. How's your bedroom?"

Lizzie twisted her lips. "There's a small fireplace but it barely penetrates the bitterness to be honest. Good job I came prepared with my water bottle and thick undies." She wiggled her eyebrows. "It's a nice temperature in here, though." She was right. Rupert had obviously made pains to install her in a warm room. It faced south and the fire was kept going day and night.

"The walls must be five feet thick," continued Lizzie as she put out the hair styling equipment.

"At least! It was a castle fort long before it was a home," Dodo explained. "Can you imagine trying to keep warm in a metal suit of armor?"

Lizzie shuddered. "At least they have electricity," she said as Dodo came to sit at the delicate Queen Anne dressing table. "And pretty decent plumbing."

Dodo ran fingers through her messy hair. "How are the staff? Friendly?"

"Very welcoming, except for the cook who is a bit of a tartar. The housekeeper hails from our neck of the woods. She invited me into her parlor for a cup of Horlicks before bed last night."

"I would imagine there will be more staff arriving today with the other guests," said Dodo as Lizzie ran a brush through her black locks.

"I've heard that the relatives are not bringing any with them, but we are expecting one other lady's maid. I hope she's not uppity."

Of course, Lizzie knew all the rules regarding her station, but so often those lines were blurred with Dodo, and she did not get along with others of her profession who were too rigid and old fashioned in their customs.

Dodo smoothed the wide legs of her dove gray, wool slacks and adjusted the ivory, argyle sweater as Lizzie dressed her hair. A beret, scarf and fur-trimmed gloves were laid out on the traditional oak, four-poster bed for later.

"Don't fuss too much with my hair as I'll be wearing a warm hat most of the day. We're going tobogganing." She ran her fingers over her earrings and necklaces but decided that they were impractical for a day of sport. She hadn't been on a sled since she was seventeen and holidayed in Switzerland right after the Great War ended. Her mother had been desperate to get away after the austere years of the conflict and so much sadness.

"That should be fun if you can keep warm," remarked Lizzie as she sprayed some lacquer over Dodo's crown.

She locked eyes with her maid. "But tonight, Lizzie, I want to look…well, I want to knock everyone's socks off." She clapped her hands to her knees. "Uphold my reputation and all that."

"That won't be a problem," declared Lizzie. "I have a lot to work with." She grinned. "Honestly, you could dress in a brown potato sack and still light up a room."

Dodo puckered her lips. "How very loyal of you, Lizzie, but there will be no potato sacks this Christmas."

Lizzie's face wrapped itself into an over-dramatic frown. "Oh dear," she cried with mock horror. "What *will* I do? I only packed sacks." She threw her hands in the air to finish the pantomime.

11

"Actually, I packed that Valérie Sourdais from Renée's collection. The black and white with the ostrich feather trim."

Dodo threw back her head. "Oh, fabulous! That should cause a stir."

At the end of a hearty breakfast Rupert asked, "Would you like an official tour of the castle?"

The pride in his expression was obvious.

"I'd love to," she said, grateful to be wearing the warm clothes Lizzie had set out.

The age and size of the building was mind-blowing compared to her own home, Beresford House, which had been built by Dodo's great-grandfather with all the 'modern' conveniences of the time. In contrast, *Knightsbrooke Priory* had originally been built with function as its driving force. The floor plan was a huge square with a tower on each corner, as might be expected in a place built primarily for defense.

The Great Hall, where they had eaten the evening before, and the drawing room were situated on the ground floor. The lack of many lights meant that when she had gone upstairs to her room the night before she had been unable to see much of the rest of the interior.

This morning, Rupert led her along a wide, high-ceilinged, upstairs passageway on the opposite side from her room, and opened an unassuming door.

To her surprise, the door opened into a bright south-facing *solar*, or family living space, bursting with reflected sunlight. The room was long and narrow with a complex vaulted roof of delicate, red wood arches. A thick, stone fireplace, topped with an intricately carved façade was centered on the wall facing the bank of windows, and feminine, floral furniture invited one to drop in and stay.

"What a marvelously unexpected room," Dodo declared, running her hand over the back of a dainty, carved chair. "I could spend a lot of time in here."

"We do. It's Mother's favorite room with so much natural light and less bulky fixtures and furnishings."

The stone window ledge was thick and padded with a deep, welcoming cushion and soft, feather pillows that made Dodo crave hot cocoa and a good book.

Rupert led her to the far side of the room where some glass panels were backed with feminine, patterned fabric. "This is my favorite part of the room." He reached up and undid a catch enabling him to pull back the screen.

Dodo gasped with utter delight as a beautiful, white stone, family chapel was revealed below.

"What a secret this room hides!" she declared leaning over to examine the small, sacred place of worship as a cold draft carrying a hint of silver polish rose from below. Eight thick, white pillars supported unmolded arches that bore carvings of thistles and leaves. Four arched windows allowed light to flood the space and bounce off the white stonework. Plain, dark wooden chairs in rows faced a simple, stone altar.

"The ancestor I spoke about, Sir Richard Danforth, took special pride in restoring the chapel. The stone was originally imported from France. It is expected that the girls will be married here."

The word 'married' bounced around the room like a rogue ping pong ball. They had only known each other for a few weeks but Dodo would be lying if she said she had never entertained the notion. Nervous to betray her thoughts she avoided his eye, instead drinking in the startling gem below.

"Your ancestor, he had a title?" she asked, since, though gentlemen, the Danforths were surprisingly devoid of any titles. Not that it mattered.

"He did," began Rupert. "But the story goes that he fell out of favor with the king over some unwanted attention he showered on the queen. He was stripped of his title and sent away from court."

Dodo turned to face Rupert with a grin. "My, my, what skeletons you *do* have."

"Are you ready to continue the tour?" Though she would have loved to linger she nodded, and he pulled back the screen, securing it with a simple locking mechanism.

They left the light airiness of the solar and walked down a dark corridor hung with heavy, dark tapestries, to one of the towers, and mounted a narrow, stone spiral staircase emerging onto the battlement. Dodo was not wearing a coat and the bitter gusts cut through her jumper, bringing tears to her eyes. Rupert wrapped an arm tightly around her shoulders, trying to protect her from the wind.

The view from here was spectacular. The sky was ice blue, the clouds from the day before sent packing by the brisk breeze. The beautiful, white landscape hugged the eye from pole to pole.

She could see a multitude of outbuildings and the twin towered gatehouse they had passed the night before. The dry moat was easily visible from here, though today instead of green it was white like everything else.

"Over there is Knight's Hill," he said pointing to a bump in the gently, undulating landscape. "That's where we'll go tobogganing." Swinging round he pointed in the other direction. "If you squint, you can see the River Soar."

The icy wind took her breath away as she peered into the wintery brightness, making her move even closer to Rupert's warmth. She could just make out the iron-colored water at a distance.

"It's a tremendous place for sailing and fishing in the summer."

He pointed to the east. "It's hard to tell today but there is a stocked lake over there where we swim and row." The top of the lake must have frozen and gathered a dusting of snow as it was completely camouflaged, and she could not distinguish it from the land. Except for a small boathouse, it would have remained undetected.

"How far does the estate extend?" she asked.

"About as far as the eye can see." Rupert pointed back in the direction of Knight's Hill. "Do you see the woods beyond the hill?"

She nodded.

"Those belong to the Priory." He turned. "See that village? It's called Chalfont Camden. The estate ends about a quarter of a mile from there." He turned again. "The river Soar is our boundary on this side." Another ninety-degree turn. "That village there is Knightsbrooke."

"Your estate is enormous!" she declared.

He wrapped her against the wind as her hair flicked and swirled into her eyes and kissed her nose. "You're cold." His face crumpled with concern.

Her fingers were beginning to go numb, and she could no longer feel her cheeks in the wind.

"We should get you inside," he declared.

She nodded and then took one last look over the edge and into the old moat.

I wonder if anyone has jumped to their death from here?

Chapter 3

Dodo and Rupert ducked back into the narrow turret tower and ran all the way down to the great hall trying to get warm. In the daylight she could see another vast fireplace with a decorated, plaster chimney piece, a delightful minstrel's gallery which had been camouflaged the day before, and several enormous, medieval tapestries hanging from the stone walls. The vaulted roof had arches made from thick beams.

"I can show you the outbuildings later when we're better protected against the elements." Rupert's eyes were shining with eagerness. Though impressive in size and age, Dodo preferred the modern comforts of her own home.

Could I end up living here? She wasn't sure how she felt about the prospect.

"Let's find the others," said Rupert leading toward the drawing room.

Everyone was in there. The usually energetic dogs were spread out by the fire, the golden one's head using the chocolate one's stomach as a pillow.

"Rupert!" cried Julia, who was wearing a particularly utilitarian skirt and jumper, with thick stockings. "Where have you been?" Her expression held a hint of friendly accusation.

The chocolate lab lifted his head in interest but decided sleep was preferable.

"I was showing Dodo the place," he replied.

"And what do you think of it?" asked Etta, her salt and peppered head tilted in expectation as she crossed her sturdy shoed feet, at the ankles.

"Rupert showed me the solar and the chapel," she said. "Absolutely breathtaking!" This was true. The other truths she felt were best kept to herself.

"That is my room," Etta said, her eyes twinkling as she smoothed the skirt of her frumpy gray dress. "When we don't have company, I spend a lot of time up there."

"Did you take her up on the roof?" asked Julia. "No tour is complete without it."

"Without a coat?" said his mother, frowning. "I should hope not!"

Rupert looked sheepish. "Yes, I did—"

"It was bracing, but I didn't mind," Dodo said quickly. "And the air was so clear we could see for miles."

"You will catch your death of cold," said Etta. "Come and sit by the fire." She seemed to have forgiven Dodo for her distasteful hobby.

"You had better get warm before we go tobogganing," said Julia, tucking her arm through Dodo's. "We will be out for hours."

"Luncheon," declared the butler who had materialized out of thin air.

Dodo pulled the soft, tight hat down over her ears as the frosty air whistled by. Her scarf was already pulled up over her mouth and the heavy lap blanket she shared with Rupert and Beatrice, lay across her knees. The virgin snow was unspoiled as they sped across its sparkling surface.

"Yippee!" cried Julia with gusto as she sat up front with the driver. "What an amazing day!" The crisp air seemed to grab her words and fling them into the perfectly blue sky.

Dodo sat between Rupert and Beatrice, whose pale face now featured some artificial color from the cold air that kissed them. She had dressed warmly for the trip, and someone had curled her thick, lustrous hair which hung in ringlets around her shoulders from under her white cap. The contrast to her gray eyes made her features pop and Dodo knew that once Beatrice was fully recovered, she could help her enhance those features to look absolutely stunning.

But right now, family and fun were the best medicine.

The old, red sleigh looked like something out of a Norman Rockwell painting she had seen in a magazine. Its cracked leather seats had been buffed and polished for the occasion and it was now flying across the snow, reminding Dodo of the Christmas

17

song. Thirty-foot fir trees dressed in pure white stood like saluting guards along their route.

Christmas spirit poured into Dodo's fertile heart and she could not stop smiling. She laid her head on Rupert's shoulder, filled with an electrifying sense of joie de vivre.

The sleigh finally slowed as the horse pulled them up Knight's Hill, his heavy hooves sliding as he tried to gain traction, eventually reaching the crest. Julia jumped down, excited as a small child, and the groom went to unload the toboggans.

"You and Rupert can take this one." Julia gasped, pointing to a sled that had rusty, iron runners, a frayed rope, and a scarred, wooden seat. "We'll take this one." She grabbed a flat-bottomed toboggan, curled at the end with a piece of twine for steering. Both had seen better days.

"I'm not sure I'm up for sledding," said Beatrice in a quiet, nervous voice.

"Nonsense!" yelled Julia. "Make her come, Rupie!"

"I think it will do you the world of good, darling," said Rupert, lifting Beatrice's still frail frame from the sleigh and setting her on the fresh snow. As she sunk into the powder a small smile stole across her plump lips.

Rupert and Julia placed each toboggan at the top of the hill and waited as Dodo and Beatrice sat on the back.

"Let's race," shouted Julia. "Ready, steady, go!"

Rupert and Julia pushed back with their heels and thrust the contraptions forward. Light snow dust fanned over Dodo's cheeks in an icy shower, melting instantly, as they careened down the slope at break-neck speed. She grabbed Rupert tightly around the waist and laid her face against his back as the wind whizzed past. The sled hit a bump causing them to lift off the seat momentarily and Dodo shrieked with delight. As they hit the flat, the sled tipped to the side and they landed in the soft powder, laughing so hard Dodo thought her ribs would crack. She stared up at the clear sky and Rupert leaned across to place cold lips on hers.

"We won!" shrieked Julia. They looked up and saw that the girls' toboggan had stopped twenty feet from where they fell. Beatrice was beaming, her whole countenance changed.

18

"Best of five," cried Rupert pulling Dodo to her feet and dragging the sled behind him.

Halfway up Beatrice's energy flagged, and Rupert turned and trudged down the hill, pulling her onto his back. Then he climbed the slope while Beatrice laughed as she bumped along.

Didi would love this!

The two siblings positioned the toboggans again.

"Go!" cried Rupert with no preamble. Dodo clasped tightly to his coat as they bumped their way down, managing to stay upright.

On this occasion it was the girls who spilled off their toboggan at the bottom, and Rupert declared he and Dodo the winners.

"That's one each," shouted Julia.

Again, Rupert carried his delicate sister up the hill leaving Dodo to appreciate the cherry redness of exertion that splashed across his jaw. Having climbed up twice herself, she tugged at her scarf, giving her neck some air.

The third race was declared a tie.

Beatrice rolled off the toboggan and lay on her back in the snow, laughing.

Glancing at Rupert, Dodo saw his eyes shining and had to bite back her own lump of emotion.

Scrambling up the hill a third time behind Rupert, Dodo saw Beatrice start to slip from his back and ran to push her back up. Now that she had climbed the hill several times, she felt really warm and was tempted to take off her coat.

Once they were situated on the brow of the hill again, Julia cried, "Go!" this time allowing Beatrice to guide the sled. Unfortunately, Beatrice proved an unreliable driver, and they flew down the hill at an angle which cost them valuable seconds.

"We won!" declared Rupert. "That's three to two."

"Only because I wasn't driving," protested Julia. "You need to let Dodo steer this time to make it fair."

Dodo was cursed with a competitive spirit given the right conditions, and she rose to the challenge. "You're on, young lady!"

Sitting atop Knight's Hill, Rupert clinging to her waist, she glared at Julia who was back in front, awaiting the call to charge.

"Ready." Julia paused, glaring at Dodo like an Old West gunslinger about to begin a duel. Dodo felt her pulse tick up.

"Steady."

Dodo set her sights on the bottom of the hill as Julia paused. "Go!"

Dodo kicked the snow with all her might, and they thrust forward, flying through the tracks they had made before, the wet dust smacking her in the face again as they flew in a straight line toward their destination, well ahead of the girls.

"Go Dodo, go!" encouraged Rupert as he held on tighter.

When they reached the bottom, the sled hit something and both Rupert and Dodo pitched headfirst over the front of the sled, landing in a tangled heap in the powdery cold.

Dodo erupted into laughter and turning her head, saw the girls take the exact same flight, thudding on their faces just a few feet from them.

"Ouch!" complained Julia through her laughter. "I think I sprained my wrist."

Rupert slithered over, using his elbows, and took his sister's hand in his, pulling off her wet mitten and gently moving the injured appendage.

"Ow!"

"I think you're right," he agreed laying her hand down. "Too bad you didn't at least win."

Julia reached out and threw snow at him with her good hand.

Rupert lifted Dodo to her feet and raising her arm in the air declared them to be the champions.

Dodo ran down the chilly stairs in a classic, ash gray day dress paired with a black and white polka dot neck scarf. Etta had explained that tea would be a much bigger feast today as dinner would be after the late carol service at the church in Knightsbrooke. As Dodo entered the room, her hair resurrected from the afternoon's activities by the talented Lizzie, she was immediately aware of a newcomer.

The woman's life was inscribed in prominent wrinkles on her sagging, aged face.

"Dodo, meet Lady Millicent Marlborough, a dear and valued friend of my mother-in-law." Etta gathered Dodo into the family group that sat around the fire drinking tea.

Lady Marlborough's white, wispy hair was pulled back in a style from the Edwardian Era that perfectly matched her attire. Dodo noted that the woman's jaw had the sunken look of someone who had lost multiple teeth. She had not aged nearly as well as Rupert's grandmother.

"Delighted," said Dodo, taking Lady Marlborough's arthritic hand.

"And you are Rupert's young lady," responded Lady Marlborough, peering into Dodo's eyes as if trying to read her mind.

"I am," she confirmed. "And very happy to have been invited for Christmas."

Rupert wandered over to take his place beside her.

"Lovely," said the old lady, her eyes gleaming as she looked at Rupert. "I can tell you a story or two about this young man," she continued with a wicked smile.

"I don't think that will be necessary, Lady Marlborough," protested Rupert.

"On the contrary," said Dodo with a wink. "I shall seek you out for a private conference as soon as maybe."

"I shall look forward to it," Lady Marlborough replied, a gnarled finger placed against her chapped lips.

Julia appeared a few minutes later, her wrist wrapped in a bandage, and kissed Lady Marlborough and her grandmother casually on the cheek. "I'm starving," she said, helping herself to some mince pies.

Beatrice arrived next looking better than Dodo had ever seen her. Her skin had color from the time outside and the long curls had survived the events of the afternoon. She had definitely turned a corner in her recovery from the opium addiction.

The door opened once more and Dodo was surprised to see a reasonably handsome young man with floppy, blond hair bounce in, smacking his hands together and blowing on them.

"Jolly cold out there!" His voice was prep-school precise.

The vicar, no doubt.

21

Julia rushed to greet him, dragging him over to the other new arrival. "Lady Marlborough, this is our new vicar, the Reverend Valentine."

He bowed low over the countess's hand and spent some minutes in polite small talk while his eyes searched the room and finally settled on a revitalized Beatrice. His friendly eyes widened in appreciation. After a few moments, he begged Lady Marlborough's pardon and went to seek out Beatrice. A light in his countenance made Dodo feel sorry for Julia.

Beatrice brightened at the approach of the young vicar and Dodo heard her whisper his Christian name, betraying an unexpected familiarity.

"What a merry party we are," declared Mrs. Danforth, like a hen gathering up her chicks. "I declare this will be a Christmas to remember. Vicar, have some pies."

He reluctantly left Beatrice in search of the Christmas delicacies.

"And what are the plans for the Christmas service this evening?" asked Adelaide Danforth from her corner of the couch.

"I am a conventional man," began the Reverend Valentine. "I am happy to follow the previous vicar's playbook at such a spiritual and sentimental time of year. Nostalgia is to be encouraged, I think. Don't you agree, Miss Danforth?"

Beatrice smiled and the natural beauty that had begun to emerge, shone forth on the vicar like the sun at midday.

Julia stared at them both.

"I do, Reverend Valentine. It is my favorite time of year."

Julia's face fell farther as she went to sit by her mother like a dog who had been reprimanded. "Can we put on some music, Mummy?"

Dodo looked around for a gramophone and spied an ancient one on a cabinet at the far end of the room.

"Of course, dear," replied her mother, barely paying attention.

Instead of jazz, the strains of classical Christmas music floated across the room adding to the festive mood.

It had not been easy to make the decision to spend Christmas away from her own family. The Dorchester's celebration was also steeped in tradition, holiday food, and friends. One of the things that had pushed her over the line was the fact that she had not yet admitted to her family her close shave with death in the last case. She had begged the Scotland Yard inspector not to name her as the kidnap victim, so the reports in the newspaper had merely made vague references to a female, to protect her identity. She needed time to distance herself from the frightening experience in order to be able to retell the story without an abundance of emotions. Rupert and Lizzie had rescued her, and she found a degree of comfort in their shared trauma without having to relive it.

But she was pleasantly surprised to find the Christmas atmosphere here at *Knightsbrooke Priory* was almost as good as her own family's, and here she didn't have to pretend or avoid awkward questions.

"I understand you and Rupert's grandmother were close friends in your youth," Dodo said to the portly Lady Marlborough.

The droopy wrinkles stretched into a squashed smile. "Inseparable, before we were married," she replied in a clipped accent. "I believe we met at three years of age and have been fast friends ever since." She smiled at Adelaide. "Though we haven't seen as much of each other of late."

"My own grandmother is fortunate enough to have similar lifelong friends," Dodo said. "They are such a comfort to her now that my grandfather has gone."

Lady Marlborough adjusted the handsome cane that lay against her leg and nodded with a knowing smile. "I take great consolation in my children and grandchildren. I live in the dower house on my son's estate," she explained. "But the root of our lasting friendship is that Adelaide was such a help when Cedric, my brother, died. We were both married by then and living far apart, but her letters were balm to my soul." The two old ladies clasped hands. "My brother and I were very close, and his death hit me hard. One might say I never recovered."

"I am so sorry to hear that," commented Dodo. "I am extremely close with my own sister. I would be devastated if anything happened to her. May I ask what happened?"

Lady Marlborough's expression became distant, her jowls dropping as she reminisced. "A few weeks after his marriage he contracted scarlet fever which developed into rheumatic fever. It damaged his heart. He was sickly for about two years and then caught the flu. His weak heart could not take it and he died." She sighed. "I was devastated, as was his poor young wife. However, she went on to remarry two years later." This last was said as a judge might declare a criminal's sentence.

"I had scarlet fever once," said Adelaide. "It was a mild case, but my skin was still red and sore. I suppose most people contract it at some point in their life."

"Does anyone want to take a stroll around the gardens?" asked Mr. Danforth, interrupting the ladies' conversation. "I need to walk the dogs and dusk hasn't quite fallen yet."

The older ladies and Rupert's sisters murmured their dissent, but Rupert raised his brows at Dodo in question. Although she had only recently warmed up from the afternoon's tobogganing, time with Rupert was at a premium and she thought it a good opportunity to get to know his father better.

"Oh, alright then," she said, wiggling her shoulders.

"Don't be late," said Rupert's mother to her husband. "I know you and your short walks. Remember we will be playing *Spoof* as usual before going to the carol service, and you will need time to change."

Spoof?

Dodo hadn't played that game in years but remembered it being a boisterous, fast card game.

She braced as she prepared to face the freezing night air.

Chapter 4

The sun hung low in the clear sky like an orange, spreading its auburn wings across the icy horizon. The air was so cold it burned Dodo's lungs. The dogs were weaving as they ran, leaving a pretty trail in the previously undisturbed snow. Their paws kicked up a spray that shone in the dimming light. Dodo laughed as the dogs stopped every so often to nuzzle the cold softness.

Though he was shorter than his son by several inches, Rupert's father was stepping out with a determined step and Dodo was almost running to catch up. She could feel her warm blood bringing much needed heat to her cold toes.

"Caught us off guard with that business about murder," he said to them, adjusting the tweed deerstalker that protected his bald head. "Your mother's brother, your uncle Oliver, died before you were born, and she blames herself for not doing more to save him. Any mention of death or murder sends her reeling for a while."

Rupert smacked his forehead with his palm. "Of course! I had forgotten. I apologize."

"It was a long time ago, and we don't talk about it. He drowned." Mr. Danforth stooped to pick up a stick. "But if you are bringing criminals to justice," he said, directing his comments to Dodo, "that is a fine calling. I just wanted to explain Etta's unusual reaction." The dogs ran back, tongues lolling out of their mouths as they panted. Mr. Danforth hurled the stick. "Now, Dodo, tell me more about your family."

Dodo was happy to oblige, and Rupert's father listened without interruption, nodding. "I think your father and I may have crossed paths in the war," he said when she was finished. "I was called to Whitehall on occasion, you know."

"Daddy too," said Dodo, her breath forming white puffs in the air.

"That must be it then. I can't tell you more than that—official secrets act." He tapped his nose with a leather-gloved finger. "But the name 'Dorchester' seemed familiar." He spun around looking for the dogs in the darkness. "Where the Dickens…? Horatio! Sabine!" Paw prints led toward a forest. "I expect they've found a squirrel. I shall have to go and get them. Tata."

Rupert put his arm around Dodo as they watched Mr. Danforth plunge into the black wilderness of trees.

"I should have remembered that about Mother," he began. "I should have warned her. Then she wouldn't have been so blindsided."

"Well, at least I know why they were so shocked," she said, feeling a little guilty for unknowingly upsetting Etta.

"But I can tell he likes you," said Rupert.

"Really? How do you know?" His father, though friendly was a little aloof.

"He walked with us for a long time. If he didn't like you he would have made some excuse to go after the dogs sooner."

The sun was now a semi-circle being consumed by the horizon, and clouds were beginning to fill the sky as night fell.

Dodo shivered.

"Let's get you back in the warm," said Rupert.

Rupert's aunt and uncle, the Quintrells, had arrived while they were gone.

"Aunt Ruby, will you allow me to introduce my girlfriend, Lady Dorothea Dorchester?"

A robust woman in her late forties, she held out a hand and shook Dodo's vigorously. "Better looking than the last one!" she wheezed with a sly smile.

Dodo felt heat rush to her cheeks, and she looked at Rupert in confusion.

"Don't mind her," said his uncle, a heavy-set man with graying red hair, slapping Rupert on the back. "Ruby left her manners back at cocktail number three."

Dodo relaxed.

Rupert twisted his lips. "Aunt Ruby is referring to Felicia Mudbuck. I was fourteen and she was twelve and she had a rather terrifying crush on me. I was always on the run from her."

"She had buck teeth, frizzy hair and rather large ears as I recall," chuckled Aunt Ruby who was no beauty herself.

Noticing their return, Mrs. Danforth said, "Oh good! Now we have plenty of people for *Spoof.*" She rang the bell for the servants to bring the card table.

After several boisterous rounds of the game that brought out quite another side of Beatrice, and a healthy amount of eggnog and candied fruit, the family dressed in their winter coats, ready to make the short journey to the village church. The hard ice crunched under foot as they stepped into a large black car. Adelaide and Lady Marlborough had decided to stay because the paths might be slippery and at their age, they couldn't be too careful. Everyone had promised to tell them all the details when they returned.

Smashed up against Rupert and Julia, Dodo faced Mr. and Mrs. Danforth and Beatrice as the grand old vehicle crept its way along the avenue to the castle and out to the village of Knightsbrooke. The Quintrells drove their own car and followed behind.

Puffy clouds were skimming across the sky, covering the moon then revealing it like a celestial sorcerer. Up ahead, Dodo could see the lights of the tiny village clinging to the valley like a garland and hear the peal of the merry bells.

The joyful memory of many other Christmases swelled in Dodo's chest, and she felt hot tears prick her eyes as she squeezed Rupert's hand.

A light snow began to fall as they approached the quaint, old church whose doors were flung open to admit the worshippers, allowing the pure sound of the choir boys to spill out into the street. A layer of pristine white blanketed the steep church roof reminding Dodo of fondant icing on rich Christmas fruit cakes.

The car slowed to a stop and the chauffeur, in his neat uniform, opened the door as the members of the Danforth family exited the vehicle. Trailing through the charming lychgate lit by lanterns, they followed the flickering candles that marked the footpath. Energetic children pushed past them laughing, unable to contain their festive-fueled excitement.

The small, plain chapel was bursting with villagers squashed shoulder to shoulder, all swaddled in thick coats and mufflers, their hats wet with melting snow.

Dodo followed the family to their row in the front and settled onto the hard bench. The dark, oak timbers that held up the roof were strung with holly, and candles stood on every available surface, shedding their soft light over the happy occasion.

Reverend Valentine stepped into the pulpit in his robes and the choir ended their carol on a high note that pierced to the very soul and echoed around the rafters.

Both Julia and Beatrice had their eyes fixed on the young cleric.

"Beloved, welcome! Good tidings and peace on earth!" he cried in a comforting baritone, as he motioned to the choir master. One solitary, clear voice began singing Once in Royal David's City and Dodo quivered with pleasure.

The familiar Nine Lessons were read by various members of the congregation as Rupert explained their roles in the village to Dodo. The mayor, the headmistress, the postmaster and members of the village council all took their turn reading. Each lesson was punctuated by beloved carols.

Dodo was pleasantly surprised to learn that Rupert had an excellent singing voice and was adept at harmonizing. Aunt Ruby on the other hand kept hiccupping and singing off key. No one batted an eye.

By the time the congregation rose to sing 'Hark! The Herald Angels Sing' with the choir, Dodo felt as though she were floating.

The spell was broken as Mr. Danforth exited the row while the organ belted out *In Dulci Jubilo.*

As Rupert's father made his way down the aisle, people reached out to wish him a merry Christmas. Saturated with Christmas cheer, Dodo smiled and nodded to every stranger she met.

The feeling of goodwill lingered as they drove back to *Knightsbrooke Priory* and after peeling off their coats in the cold foyer, they found sanctuary in the cheery drawing room. Here, more eggnog awaited them beside the roaring fire. Dodo noticed Lawrence Quintrell less than subtly discouraging his wife from imbibing.

The two widows were already dressed in their Christmas finery, Adelaide in a dramatic velvet gown with a daring turban and Lady Marlborough in a heavy silver taffeta. Their expressions evidenced that they were awaiting the church party's return, eager to hear everything. Everyone paid the two grand ladies court, recounting the church service in delightful detail.

After several minutes, Etta announced that dinner would be served in half an hour and Dodo excused herself to get dressed.

Rupert caught up, entangling his fingers with hers and pulling her under some mistletoe that had been hung in a dark corner of the hallway. She giggled as he drew her close against his warm chest, tilting his head and leaning to within a whisker of her lips. Her blood leapt in response as she closed her eyes in anticipation of the explosion of feelings his kiss would set off.

Nothing.

Opening her eyes, he had not moved, his lips close, energy humming between them like a forcefield. She searched his eyes that danced with playfulness, seeing flecks of pure white spiraling the brilliant blue.

She caught her breath.

A smile began to creep over his face, and she ached for their lips to touch.

Heat rose in her veins.

Kiss me, you fool!

Suspended in time, she felt dizzy with impatience and emotion, but thrilled by the effect he had on her.

This was what she had yearned for.

Softly, he pressed his lips to hers and a blissful happy belonging filled her.

"You made me wait," she murmured when he pulled away.

"Yes."

"For the record, it was worth it."

"How was the service?" asked Lizzie when Dodo eventually made it up to her room. At Beresford House, Lizzie was included in the Christmas Eve Service and Dodo was acutely aware that missing this tradition would hit her hard. But none of the staff from *Knightsbrooke Priory* attended. Not only was Lizzie unable to be with her own family, she had also been unable to sing the carols she loved.

"It was beautiful. Perhaps even better than in Little Puddleton," Dodo admitted.

"Praise indeed," said Lizzie helping her out of her warm clothes and wrapping her mistress in a silk robe.

"I'm sorry you had to miss it."

"Not to worry. I got my fill. The housekeeper played the piano, and we all sang to our hearts content. Everyone but Lady Marlborough's maid, that is."

"Oh, I am glad you got to sing, but it's not quite the same," said Dodo, tying the robe. "So, the newly arrived maid is not sociable?"

Lizzie's brows raised. "That's an understatement. She gave us all the evil eye with pursed lips and then demanded to be taken to her room. We hardly saw her after that. Just as well if you ask me. She would have put a damper on the festivities."

Dodo moved away from the dressing table and found something in her handbag which she proudly presented to Lizzie.

"I know what a sacrifice it was to come with me for Christmas," she explained, offering the little package to her maid. "So, I hope this will make up for it in a small way and show my appreciation. Merry Christmas!"

Lizzie's eyes widened and darted from the box to Dodo's face. "Whatever…" she began taking the little, blue box. Prying it open she gasped. "Oh, m'lady, you shouldn't have."

"Yes, I should," contradicted Dodo. "You have done so much for me this year and I know how much you love the Christmas service. I had to do something to compensate for having to miss it."

Lizzie withdrew a fine gold chain with a perfect, ivory pearl hanging from its middle.

"Here, let me put it on you." Dodo took the chain and laid it around Lizzie's neck. It sat perfectly just below the nape. Lizzie's fingers went to it, feeling the smoothness of its surface, her eyes glistening.

"Go and take a look in the mirror," ordered Dodo, clasping her hands under her chin.

Lizzie did as she was bid. "Thank you, m'lady. I can honestly say I have never had anything so priceless as this. I'll wear it when I get married."

Dodo hugged her. "That is a great compliment," she said. "Now, I'd better get ready."

The black and white dress from the House of Dubois was the latest style. It hung where it could and clung where it should. When Rupert clapped eyes on her the change in his expression was all the encouragement she needed to feel that she had chosen the right gown. A secret hung in the air between them.

"Oh, Dodo!" cried Julia, who was wearing a hideous shiny, green dress with an undesirable bow above her bottom. "You look magnifique! Look Mummy, doesn't Dodo look incredible?"

Mrs. Danforth was wearing a silver gray, long gown gathered at the bust with black beads around the neck. It was understated and…safe.

"My, oh my," said Adelaide, admiring Dodo's gown. "I have never seen anything quite so… stunning. The ostrich complements the lines of the fabric so well. And the bandeau is to die for."

"You look lovely," said Mrs. Danforth, kissing Dodo on the cheek.

"Thank you."

Rupert crossed the room to claim her. "I was enjoying the view from a distance," he said with a glint of desire in his blue eyes.

Dodo glanced around and spied Beatrice. Though her dress was understated like her mother's, her hair was up, tucked under a jeweled headband. She looked fabulous and Dodo told her so.

"Dinner is served." As usual for their type, the butler had managed to enter the room noiselessly.

"Perfect timing," Rupert whispered in a sultry tone that caused her heart to skid across her chest.

Tonight, the enormous, impersonal dining hall was illuminated with a hundred or more candles, giving the harsh space a festive softness.

As they were waiting for instructions, the vicar slipped in. Dodo's eyes went to Beatrice and Julia whose faces brightened at his entrance.

"Etta will sit at the bottom of the table, and I will sit at the top," pronounced Mr. Danforth. "But since it is Christmas, the rest of you may sit where you wish."

The vicar side-stepped arriving beside Beatrice.

Julia's smile lost its luster.

Adelaide and Lady Marlborough sat opposite Dodo and Rupert, with Julia opposite the vicar next to Rupert, and the Quintrells split on either side of the table.

"Beautiful service, vicar," said Etta as the game soup was served.

The young cleric's spoon hovered over his bowl. "Didn't want to make any waves. As I said, I may be young, but I understand that people appreciate tradition at Christmas."

"The boy who sang the solo was exquisite," said Beatrice with more animation than Dodo had seen in all the time she had known her.

Dodo saw gratification suffuse the vicar's boyish features like a magician's bouquet being revealed from under a hat. Julia looked prickly as a thistle.

"Tommy Tucker—such a find but we were worried his voice would break before the service," explained the vicar. "He grew two inches in the last month. It's been touch and go."

"I wish I could have heard him," said Adelaide with a curious wink at the vicar.

The guests around the table began to speak quietly to their neighbors and Dodo poured herself some water from a carafe. She had already reached her limit of alcohol for the evening.

32

Adelaide licked her dry lips. "Tell me more about the murders, Lady Dorothea."

Her voice had been low, but the comment had attracted the attention of her son. "Not now, Mother," pronounced Rupert's father from the end of the table. "Not suitable dinner talk, in my opinion." He shot a worried glance at his wife who took a quick gulp of wine and for a moment the air sizzled with tension.

Adelaide's face screwed up in disappointment and she whispered, "I shall expect a detailed account after dinner in the drawing room."

Dodo smothered a chuckle and nodded.

For the rest of the course, Adelaide chatted quietly with Lady Marlborough.

The second dish was white fish baked to perfection with a plum sauce that had Dodo wishing she could get the recipe for the cook at home. Then a large roast goose was brought in with great pomp and ceremony.

The creamed parsnips were light and fluffy and the roast potatoes crisp and hot. Dodo was beginning to wonder if she should have chosen a gown with more room to breathe.

Glancing across the table she saw Adelaide dabbing at her forehead and drinking from a clandestine glass of eggnog.

"Is this the kind of feast you would have at home?" asked Rupert sneaking a hand onto her lap.

"We would probably have trout and turkey," she said. "My father is partial to trout."

"I hope you are not missing it." He smiled.

"Not at all I—"

"Ahhh!"

She was cut short as Adelaide produced an odd choking sound, clutching her throat. Dodo watched in horror as Rupert's grandmother gasped for breath then keeled over, face first into the parsnips.

"Mother!" cried Mr. Danforth, jumping up to go to her aid as the rest of the table remained frozen in their seats, gaping in terror at the still form.

Before Mr. Danforth could reach her, Lady Marlborough reached over a finger to search for a pulse.

She blinked like a barn owl.

"She's dead."

Chapter 5

Dodo observed the people at the table become suspended in a frozen tableau of shock and disbelief while warning bells started clanging in her head.

Julia and Beatrice sat like marble statues, their mouths open in terror. All color drained from Etta's face as she stared straight ahead, avoiding the ugly sight before her.

Mr. Danforth leaned over his mother's still form and felt for a pulse himself.

"It's true."

Dropping to his knees he rested his head briefly on her shoulder as Lady Marlborough covered her face with a serviette.

As if a stage director had waved an arm for the action to resume, the vicar pushed back his chair and stood. "May I offer my condolences to everyone." He bestowed a look of pity on the family. "And may I suggest moving the dear lady upstairs?"

"I suppose…we should do that," stuttered Mr. Danforth, wiping his eye. "I dare-say it was just her time."

Dodo stood, spurred by experience and a nagging doubt as to the truth of Mr. Danforth's words. It was imperative that she get a good look at the body before it was moved to dispel her fears. Poor Adelaide's head was still face-down in the creamed parsnip and Dodo used the opportunity of restoring dignity to the dead woman, to examine her.

Without asking permission, Dodo briskly walked around the table while the others were still reacting, and the men were discussing how best to carry Adelaide upstairs. She gently lifted Adelaide's face from the plate and wiped the bright skin clean from food as her eyes took in every detail. She desperately wanted this to be an untimely natural death, but a slight white foam at the corner of Adelaide's mouth and her heightened color told a different story.

She leaned down and breathed in. *Bitter almonds!*

Shocked, she pretended to wipe imaginary food from the dead woman's face to confirm her conclusion. The acrid smell of bitter almonds was faint but definitely present.

Cyanide.

If Dodo was hoping to win over Rupert's mother after a rocky start, this situation would all but close that door. She must contact the police.

"That is so kind of you," said Rupert's father from behind her. "We can take it from here." She stepped back as the men gathered the dead woman in their arms, anxious that a murdered corpse was being moved before the police arrived. She clenched her fists and snapped her eyes shut in an effort to stamp the murder scene in her brain.

"Someone should call the police," she declared with more confidence than she felt.

"Police?" said Lawrence, his face confused. "Wouldn't a doctor or an undertaker be more appropriate?"

"I believe it is protocol to inform the police whenever someone dies," she said, emphatically. "I would be happy to do that."

Rupert's mother stirred, her face as white as her dead mother-in-law's should be, and flicked her napkin in the air. "Yes, yes," she said absently. "Someone should."

Dodo took the comment as the authority she needed and after asking a dazed footman where the telephone was, slipped quickly from the room.

"Police station," she stated to the operator.

"Putting you through."

"Knightsbrooke Police Station. How can I help you?" The sleepy voice on the other end was very young and Dodo realized that on the Christmas Eve graveyard shift, the lowest man on the totem pole would have drawn the short straw.

She spoke in a clipped tone, exaggerating her already plummy accent. "This is Lady Dorothea Dorchester. I am up at *Knightsbrooke Priory* with the Danforths and there has been a death." She didn't want to use the word 'murder' just yet and send him into a panic.

A subtle shift in the young constable's voice indicated that he was now wide awake. "A death? Who is the deceased person?"

"It is Mr. Danforth's mother, Adelaide Danforth."

"Oh," replied the constable, resuming the relaxed, almost bored tone. "She was a *very* old lady, I understand, so it is not totally unexpected."

"It is true that she was old," agreed Dodo, "but I happened to be close to the body and I believe she may have been poisoned with cyanide."

There was a pause on the other end of the telephone. "And how would you know that, if you don't mind me asking?"

Dodo took a deep breath. "I have some experience in the matter—"

"You have experience poisoning people?" asked the constable.

"No, of course not! I was going to say that I have some experience with investigating murders, and I can tell you the smell of bitter almonds was present, her skin was red, and there was some white foam around the deceased's mouth."

"Well, I'm blowed!" said the constable. "Fancy you knowing that."

"Shall you send an inspector to the house?" she persisted. "The body has already been moved and no one else knows what I have just told you. Someone should come as soon as possible."

The constable hesitated again. "Well, er, it's almost two o'clock in the morning on Christmas…"

Dodo was losing patience. "I am telling you that the old lady was murdered. Wake up your inspector immediately. I shall be waiting." She hung up on the policeman to underline the seriousness of the matter.

Preserve the scene.

Running back to the dining room she saw that all the ladies were still there, dazed and numb. Dodo rushed to the place Adelaide had lately been while everyone remained in a shocked stupor, whisked the plate and crystal glass off the table and wrapped them in a napkin.

"What are you doing?" asked a confused Lady Marlborough, her wrinkled features like a topographical map.

"Nothing," she lied. "I'm just being extra cautious. I am sure the doctor will want to know what she was eating when she died."

The old lady frowned and shook her head, tut tutting. Ignoring her, Dodo flew out of the room and up the stairs, ostrich feathers flying in the breeze. She entered her room and rang the bell. While she waited for Lizzie, she sniffed the food and glass.

Nothing.

She had read that it could take up to fifteen minutes for cyanide to do its work, but she was no expert. When could it have been administered if not in the food and wine? She thought back to Adelaide swabbing her head when the goose was served, no longer engaging in the conversation. Maybe she was already suffering from the effects of the poison.

Think, think.

Why would someone want to kill a harmless ninety-five-year-old widow? Money? Jealousy? Revenge?

Lizzie eventually appeared in her nightgown, rags twisted in her honey hair.

"Are you ill m'lady?" she asked, her voice heavy with sleep and her eyes drooping.

"No! Adelaide Danforth died during dinner."

Lizzie's hand flew to her mouth. "That's awful!" she cried.

"It gets worse," Dodo announced. "I believe she was murdered."

Fatigue disappeared from Lizzie's features like dew on a mid-summer morning. "Murdered? How?"

"I examined the body and smelled cyanide."

Lizzie's eyes grew wide. "Poison? Why on earth would someone murder an old lady at Christmas of all times?"

"That is the question, my dear Watson."

Lizzie's eyes snapped up to her mistress. "Do you really think of me as your Watson?"

"You are much better than stodgy old Watson, my dear."

Lizzie looked like she had won first prize at the county fair. "That's maybe the nicest thing anyone has ever said to me," she said. "Has anyone called the police?"

"I have, though they only had one young constable on duty."

"Well, it *is* the middle of the night on Christmas Eve," pointed out Lizzie. "I'm sure their best people have the night off."

Dodo sighed. "That was obvious when I called. Which is why I immediately ran back to preserve the evidence." She pointed to the glass and plate. "Who knows when the police will get here? And the fact that she was so old will no doubt cause them to dillydally." She drew a finger across her sculpted eyebrow. "I have to confess that I cannot smell cyanide in either of these, but I need to safeguard them for the police to test. I did swipe the napkin I used to wipe her mouth and you can smell it faintly on there." She pushed her hands up her face, dislodging the bandeau. "I haven't told anyone else of my suspicions, but I needed to retrieve them before the servants cleared the table and washed away the evidence." She looked up. "That's why I called you. I need something to put them in."

"Let me see if I can find a glass container with a lid in the kitchen." Lizzie headed for the door.

"I am sure it goes without saying, but don't mention this to anyone yet. I don't want the murderer to be alerted to the fact that I know. Make up a story if anyone finds you poking about in the kitchen."

Lizzie tapped the side of her nose. "Of course, m'lady."

Dodo began pacing, her brain firing on all pistons, when there was a knock on her door.

"Dodo?"

"Oh, Rupert. Come in, come in."

"Julia said you ran out of the dining room. Is everything alright?"

She turned to him with strained eyes. "No, everything is not alright."

"Someone dying right in front of you is pretty frightful," he said reaching for her hand.

She pulled it away. "It's not that."

His features hardened as he looked at her. "Tell me," he said. "I can handle it."

"You might want to sit down," she said, leading him to the twin wing-back armchairs next to the fireplace.

When he was settled, his hands gripping the arms of the chair she said, "There is no easy way to say this; your grandmother was murdered."

Rupert made a short, barking laugh, heavy with incredulity. "Dodo, she was ninety-five. It was just her time. Don't you think you are seeing murders everywhere?"

A sliver of irritation reared its head, but she pushed it down. He did not yet know what she knew.

"I believe she was killed with cyanide."

That wiped the grin off his handsome face. "You're serious."

She raised a brow. "To risk a pun, deadly."

She explained about the odor of bitter almonds that still lingered on the serviette, that she had smelled coming from his grandmother's mouth, the cherry red of her skin and the slight agitation she had noticed in his grandmother's behavior during dinner.

He ran his hands through his hair. "Crikey! That does put a different spin on things."

She reached forward. "That is the real reason I called the police. I'm hoping they'll be here soon."

A wave of anger passed over his face. "Whatever reason would someone have to do this?"

"That is the question." She locked eyes with him. "You mentioned that your grandmother is a very wealthy woman who likes to change her will."

A look of scorn crossed his face. "She was just blowing hot air, Dodo. If she did change anything, it was likely small bequests to servants and the like."

Dodo could hear movement downstairs. The shock must be wearing off and people were moving around. "Do you know that for a fact? Did she ever say that to you?"

'Well, no but what else could it be?" Rupert's brow knitted in disbelief.

She thought for a minute. "Christmas will delay everything. The funeral and the reading of the will may not be for a few days. We should try and find out if she promised anyone anything. Did she tell you if you were a beneficiary?"

He shrugged. "I don't know. I've never really thought about it."

Dodo huffed. "Because you don't need it," she said. "But is it likely to be you?"

"I suppose so, and some money for the girls and other grandchildren. Why?"

"Because we need to search for a motive." Dodo tapped her lip. "Does your grandmother have any enemies?"

Another knock on the door interrupted them. She jumped up to get it and found a rather disheveled maid holding a brass bucket.

"Yes?"

"Beggin' your pardon, m'lady, but I was sent to see if you needed the fire stoked."

Dodo looked at the grate where her fire had burned down to the embers. "That might be a good idea. I shall be up for a few hours yet."

She opened the door to let the girl in, as the maid covered her mouth to hide a yawn. She kneeled by the fire and placed two large logs on the cinders.

"Wishing you a 'Merry Christmas' doesn't seem quite right," Dodo said to the maid as she left, but I shall do it all the same."

"Thank you m'lady."

"Now where were we?" she asked Rupert.

"You were asking if Grandmother had any enemies. She was ninety-five, even if she did, they would probably be dead already."

"This is a mind-boggler." She crossed her legs and smoothed the gorgeous gown which now seemed wildly impractical. "Tell me about your aunt and uncle."

Rupert's eyes became guarded. "Are you suggesting that Aunt Ruby would kill her own mother?"

Dodo leveled her gaze at Rupert. His naivete was endearing. "Not really, I just like to have as much information about everyone as I can."

He crossed his arms. "Well, she's a couple of years younger than my father, they have four children who are grown and gone, and they live in a glorified cottage by the sea. Uncle Lawrence was a fourth son and there was very little money to go around."

41

So, they need money.

"What about the Reverend Valentine?"

Rupert's eyes bugged. "The vicar is a suspect?"

Dodo couldn't help but chuckle. "Darling, everyone is a suspect until proven innocent, in my eyes."

He stood and pulled her to her feet, encircling her waist with his arms. "Am I a suspect again?"

She walked her fingers up his chest until they were on his bottom lip. "Suspect number one."

He grabbed her hand in his then leaned in for a kiss.

"Oh, excuse me!" Lizzie did an about turn.

"No, no, come back," said Dodo, stepping out of Rupert's arms.

Lizzie reluctantly walked back in. "I found this." She held out a bell jar, her cheeks a telltale shade of pink.

"Perfect."

Lizzie was hanging near the door, eyes cast down, fingers picking at the rags in her hair, clearly embarrassed for Rupert to see her in her nightgown.

"I think we should go down and mingle with everyone who is still up," Dodo said, looking at Rupert. "Perhaps we can learn some things."

"I don't know," said Rupert with uncharacteristic hesitation. "You are basically saying that one of my family members killed my grandmother."

Dodo stood firm, arms akimbo. "Murder is an ugly business, but the perpetrator must be brought to justice whoever they may be. We will follow where the truth leads, and we must be courageous if it doesn't end well."

Rupert cracked his knuckles. "Who do you really suspect?"

She swept the room with an arm. "No one…and everyone. Right now, all we have is a murder victim and a houseful of people. I make it a habit not to jump to conclusions."

"I'm not sure I have the nerve for it," he said. "Even though this is the third murder I've been involved in, when it hits so close to home it makes my stomach turn."

She patted his arm. "I know it's awful darling, but I won't tell anyone of my suspicions before the police arrive. I'll let *them* reveal the sad news. Let's just console people and see what emerges."

"Will you need me, m'lady?" asked Lizzie who was still by the door.

"Not until the police get here and who knows when that will be? Go back to bed."

A clock struck three.

Lizzie slid from the room and Rupert returned to the drawing room while Dodo changed into something more practical.

When she arrived downstairs, she was surprised to see several people comforting each other. The fire had died down and the room held a definite chill. Rupert went to find some wood.

Etta was holding her daughters close, a look of quiet despair on her face. Dodo believed it was from the shock of watching someone die in front of her. Most people were saved from witnessing such a sordid event.

What would *her* revelation do to them?

She glanced around the room. Aunt Ruby was alone, nursing a brandy while staring, without seeing, into the fire. Dodo took a seat beside her.

"I'm so sorry," she began. "Losing one's mother must be extremely difficult."

'What?" Ruby was clearly three sheets to the wind as she tried to focus on Dodo. "Oh, yes. Terrible. But not totally unexpected. She was ninety-five after all. 'Three score years and ten' is what it tells us in the bible. That's why we decided to spend Christmas with her. You never know when it might be her last."

Ruby wiped her cheeks and went back to staring into the fire.

"Still, to have it happen right in front of you is quite shocking," pushed Dodo.

"Now that, yes. I have never seen anyone die before. Dreadful! I fear I will never be able to erase that picture from my mind." She locked bloodshot eyes on Dodo. "My husband's father died two years ago but we weren't there, and he died in his sleep. That's how I want to go. I can't get the way Mother clutched her throat out of my head." She shivered. "It wasn't a peaceful passing, was it?"

Her eyes were shadowed with horror, and she took another swig of the brandy.

"Mother had mentioned that she changed her will in our favor. Thankfully she had already done it…at least I trust she had."

Chapter 6

"What?" Ruby's comment grabbed Dodo's attention.

Ruby kept her eyes on the fire. "Yes, I daresay it's crass to be thinking of that now but we have been going through some financial difficulties and Mother was so understanding. Said she was going to change the will so that we got a greater share of the pie. We are rather depending on it." She raised sheepish eyes. "I expect you think badly of me for talking of money at such a time as this, but we are in dire need. It's just a shame I had to lose my mother to be relieved of the debt." She stared back into the flames, deep in thought and Dodo decided she was unlikely to get more out of her at the moment. She would make a note of this fact and investigate it further at a later time.

Lady Marlborough was still up, sitting apart from the family group like a giant bulldog, dabbing her eyes with a handkerchief. Dodo took the seat next to her.

"My condolences on the loss of your friend," she began. "You two must have been through so much together."

"Yes," she said as she wiped her nose. "Adelaide was my daughter's godmother."

"That tells me a great deal," remarked Dodo.

Her corrugated face furrowed further with grief. "We even came out together, you know. My husband had his eye on Adelaide first, but they were not a good match. He was far too serious for her. I owe my marriage and my title to Adelaide as I offered consolation when she rejected him." Her glistening cheeks gleamed in the low candlelight.

"Will you stay for the funeral then? I fear it will be delayed because of Christmas," said Dodo.

"I have nowhere to be," said Lady Marlborough, tucking her handkerchief into a pretty jeweled bag. "If the family doesn't mind, I shall."

"It's a great shame I had so little time to become acquainted with her," continued Dodo, hoping to keep the old lady talking for a little longer.

Lady Marlborough nodded. "You would have come to love her. She was a kind and generous soul. She may not have had a title, but her husband had a tidy fortune that he invested well." She waved a beringed hand at Dodo. "She loaned my William, the present Lord Marlborough, some money after a speculation went bad and he wangled an invitation to a royal event she was interested in. After the event she forgave the loan. Not too many people are that free with their money. She recently told me that he had a special place in her heart in consequence of his actions and that he would be named as a beneficiary in her will. What generosity."

Indeed!

The back of the old lady's hand came up to stop a sob and Dodo thought it prudent to let the old lady grieve in private.

As she turned to move, the vicar walked back into the room, radiating spiritual energy. "I have prayed over the body to send the spirit of the dear departed Mrs. Danforth into the eternities."

"Thank you, vicar," said Rupert's father as he placed an arm around his increasingly fragile wife.

The Reverend Valentine cast a furtive glance at Beatrice who was still enfolded in her mother's embrace and then strode to take a seat on the other side of the room.

Dodo followed.

"Have you performed many death-bed prayers?" she asked him. "I understand you are quite new to the area."

His frank, friendly face looked up. "Yes, but I was a curate in Hampshire for four years before coming here. The congregation was elderly, and we seemed to have at least one death a month. I think it is safe to say that I have performed more prayers over the dead than marriages, actually." His eyes flicked to Beatrice again when he said the word 'marriage'.

"And how long have you been here in Knightsbrooke?"

"Almost a year. I arrived just after Christmas. Miss Beatrice had recently returned from finishing school. She made me feel at home right away. She has a way of doing that." His lovesickness was beginning to grate on Dodo. She doubted very much that he was the Danforth's idea of a good match for their eldest daughter.

"Then you have the advantage of me," she said. "I do not know Beatrice very well yet." She stole a peek at Rupert. "But I hope to get to know her better."

The vicar smiled knowingly. "Please don't form your opinion of her at the moment, she has been ill of late, and it has stolen her youthful ebullience."

"Do you know what ails her?" Dodo was interested to know if the vicar knew of her addiction to opium.

"I don't know the details, but youth is vigorous, and I'm sure she will bounce back soon."

It was time to turn the conversation in a different direction. "How well did you know the deceased?"

The vicar scratched his neck. "Very well, actually. She would call me for confession, and I would come to the house given her advanced age. She would talk for hours, and I was only too happy to listen."

"But you must be so busy. I'm surprised you could spare the time," said Dodo.

"There was something *special* about Adelaide Danforth." He dropped his voice. "She asked me to perform a little commission for her just this summer and to show her thanks she altered her will to benefit the church. So generous! We are in need of a new roof, more electric lighting as well as heat. She told me in the strictest confidence, of course, but now that she has passed away, I see nothing wrong in telling you. It will be public knowledge soon enough." He clasped his hands, brows raised in hopeful arcs.

Dodo tried to control the surprise from showing on her face. Just how many people had the old lady promised money to? It was looking more and more as though Adelaide may have been killed to prevent her changing her will yet again.

Beatrice stood to get some water from the sideboard and the vicar's head swiveled to follow her. "If you will excuse me Lady Dorothea."

Dodo nodded and felt the weight of fatigue hit her.

She looked around the room. Julia was watching the pair of sweethearts with a pained expression, Etta Danforth was still descending into depression, Rupert's father was attending to the fire, and his aunt and uncle were huddled in private conversation with serious faces. Rupert was sitting with Lady Marlborough whose tears were still streaming down her face.

Could one of these people be a killer?

The room was so quiet that Dodo heard someone arrive at the front door. The dogs, who were sleeping together by the fire, raised their heads as one, lifting their ears, determining whether the newcomer was friend or foe. After several seconds, their snouts dropped back to their paws, but their eyes stayed open, darting around the space.

"Inspector Allingham," announced the butler, showing the inspector into the room. The dogs barked once sharply but Mr. Danforth commanded them to be quiet and they obeyed.

Rupert's father stalked toward him. "Good evening, Inspector. I am the deceased's son."

"No need for introductions," said the inspector through a stiff, wiry mustache. "I know exactly who you are, sir."

"Excuse me for appearing indelicate but, are the police in the habit of sending a senior officer to every death in the county?" Rupert's father had a look of genuine bewilderment on his face.

The inspector's square head looked as if it had been fashioned by an amateur sculptor. Dodo watched as his small eyes scanned the room, finally settling on her. She gave an imperceptible shake of her head and he looked away.

The inspector took a moment then said, "It is not sir, but since you are the most prominent family in the area we wanted to go above and beyond. We take care of those who take care of us."

"That is very good of you," said Rupert's father.

Dodo happened to drop her gaze to Etta who was staring daggers at her, accusation flaming in her eyes. Dodo looked away.

Oh, dear!

An uncomfortable pit opened its mouth wide in her stomach and she hoped the inspector would not call her out and fan the flames of Mrs. Danforth's suspicion.

"If you could take me to the body and then to the scene of the…uh…incident."

Thank goodness! A discreet policeman.

Dodo found Rupert who was also studying his mother. Could he see the animosity building toward Dodo as she could?

Etta finally dropped her eyes to the rug.

As Mr. Danforth and the inspector left, Rupert came over to Dodo. "I must apologize for my mother. She is simply troubled because of the bad memories this rakes up. You saw how she was when I mentioned your sleuthing and then you made that joke about death following you, well, she's more than a little superstitious. And she hates the police and now they are here."

Dodo sliced the air with a hand. "But she's correct, isn't she? It does follow me. I suspected foul play and I was right. And it is I who have involved the police. I fear this will not turn the tide in my favor."

"She'll come around." Rupert leaned his head against hers but the pit remained wide open.

Ten minutes later the inspector returned.

"Good evening. I should like to question everyone, just to cross the t's and dot the i's." His small, black eyes snapped to hers. "Lady Dorothea, perhaps you would indulge me by being my first witness."

"Of course." She crossed the rug, weariness forgotten, and together they went to a room she had never entered. It was made of the same thick, gray stone walls as most of the other rooms but was hung with maps on the one wall that was not covered by enormous bookshelves. Mr. Danforth's study.

The smell of tobacco hung in the air, which was surprising because she had not seen Rupert's father smoke since she arrived.

"Please, take a seat, Lady Dorothea." The inspector sat on one side of the most ornate desk she had ever seen. The sides were intricate wood carvings depicting a crest of some kind and bookended with carved lion's heads. The top was smooth with a delicately carved border. It was a stunning work of art and was probably worth more money than the inspector earned in ten years.

"I wanted to thank you for not landing me in the soup in there," began Dodo. "I am trying to make a good impression."

"I pride myself in my ability to be tactful," he began. "And I gather that you are not interested in being the bearer of the bad news that Adelaide Danforth was murdered."

"No! And I appreciate your delicacy, inspector. I am a relative stranger to the family and would hate to blot my copybook by announcing that their beloved grandmother was poisoned and likely by someone in the room."

He chuckled. "I can well imagine that would not go down well." He laced his thick fingers together on the top of the desk. "Having seen the body I can tell you that I could no longer smell the cyanide, though her skin is still very red, and someone has wiped the froth away."

"That was me. I still have the napkin I used," she admitted.

"Good. I think the lab people can test the fabric for the poison. And of course, there is your testimony which I assume you would be prepared to swear to in court."

"Absolutely! My maid is a second witness too."

"Splendid." He twirled a pencil between his fingers. "How do you think the poison was administered?"

"At first I thought it might have been put in her food or wine. I collected the glass and plate from the room before the servants cleared the table—they are also in my room. But the distinctive odor was not apparent."

The inspector opened his notebook. "Did Mrs. Adelaide Danforth attend the church service?"

"With the snow and the possibility of ice, she and Lady Marlborough decided to stay home."

He looked up. "So, it was a last-minute decision?"

"Yes. I hadn't thought of that." She leaned her chin on her palm. "The murderer could not have known that she would make that decision. But poison does require some pre-meditation, wouldn't you agree?"

"I would." He tilted his square head. "If you don't mind me saying so, m'lady, you appear to have a lot of know-how about police procedure."

Dodo affected a look of bashful modesty. "I have worked a few cases in my day...and alongside Scotland Yard from time to time."

The stout face registered surprise. "That would explain it then." He drew a finger along a bushy eyebrow. "With it being Christmas and us being low-staffed, I would appreciate your assistance, if you could give it, m'lady."

Now Dodo was the one who was surprised. Usually, the local constabulary bristled at her interference. "I would be delighted, but I will take a low-key approach, if you don't mind. As I mentioned, this is the first time I have met the family and I am trying not to make waves as the son of the household is my current beau. I am afraid that if I take a more formal role, I may ostracize them."

"Right you are," agreed the inspector.

"I shall certainly continue to talk to the members of the household and report back to you in private. Does that suit?"

"I am sure that will work just fine," he assured her. "People are more likely to make mistakes if they are off their guard, anyway. Formal interviews make people very cagey about what they disclose."

"I did try to talk to everyone in the drawing room before you arrived." She leaned forward noticing the chill in the air. "It may interest you to know that Adelaide had told several people they would be major beneficiaries in her will."

The inspector's beady eyes widened. "That *is* interesting."

"She appears to have used the lure of her wealth to steer people into doing her bidding."

"Is that so? That tells us a little about her character. Crafty!" He wiggled the sausage-like fingers. "So, each of these people expect to become wealthy now that she is dead. That should cause a few fireworks."

"My thoughts exactly, but it gets even more interesting," she explained, rubbing her arms for warmth. "Yesterday evening, as she sat by the fire, she dropped off to a restless sleep and murmured something about changing her will. I asked Rupert about it, and he said she was always threatening to do it. So much so that the family never took it seriously." She looked pointedly at the solid inspector.

He pointed the pencil at her. "Perhaps someone did take her seriously and stopped her before she could do it."

"Exactly."

She realized she was tense all over from the chilly air. A fire had been lit but the heat had not made much headway.

"This is excellent intelligence, m'lady."

"Thank you, Inspector," she said, crossing her arms. "And I thought I might have my maid question the kitchen staff by way of conversation to see if anything unusual happened before we left for the Christmas service or while we were gone. She is adept as such things."

He tapped the beautiful scrollwork on the desk. "Being short-handed, I will gladly take you up on that."

She crossed her legs and clasped her arms around them. "May I ask how you intend to inform the family that their matriarch was murdered?"

He scratched his gray, thatched head. "You think I need to tread gently?"

"I do. Besides the fact that it is Christmas, Mrs. Danforth is very sensitive to the subject of death, let alone murder."

"How about after all the interviews, I make a low-key announcement tomorrow that things are not as clear cut as we first thought? We try to treat the gentry with kid gloves as it is. Mr. Danforth is good to the village and the county. Generous with his means and his time. Don't need to put the cat among the pigeons any sooner than is necessary."

"I believe that is a wise decision. As I said, Mrs. Danforth is very shaken by events. She apparently has a history with unexpected deaths that unsettles her to this day."

"Oh?"

"Rupert's father told me that her brother died young, and she blames herself. He drowned."

"I shall see if I can find anything about it in the archives. You never know, it might have a bearing on tonight's events. Do you happen to know her maiden name?"

Her teeth began to chatter. "No, I'm sorry but I can ask Rupert. He knows that this is a murder investigation."

"Right. I can ask Mrs. Danforth herself during the interview, too."

A knock on the door interrupted them and Rupert poked his head around the door.

"Lady Marlborough has fainted."

Chapter 7

Dodo and the inspector locked eyes.

Or has she been poisoned!

As Dodo and the inspector rushed into the dim, warm drawing room, a crowd had gathered around the ninety-five-year-old Lady Marlborough who was reclining on one of the sofas.

She's alive!

Dodo let out a breath when she saw that the old lady had been revived with smelling salts.

It was now nearing four o' clock in the morning and the strain of travel, the shock of her friend's death, and the late hour had clearly contributed to the elderly lady's condition.

"Let's get Lady Marlborough up to her room," Inspector Allingham suggested. "I can interview her tomorrow."

As for the other family members and guests, the inspector called them one by one.

When Rupert returned from his father's study, he wore a wry smile.

"For a country bumpkin he's not a bad policeman," he declared. "Asked me some very sensible questions but I wasn't able to be of much use."

"Tut, tut," said Dodo wagging her finger. "I thought you would have learned by now that one never knows what information might be relevant."

"Duly noted." Rupert settled back into the sofa and stifled a yawn. "Father Christmas won't be making an appearance here tonight."

She leaned against him, fighting a yawn herself. "Perhaps not, but he has paid me a visit already."

"Really?"

"Yes, my family gave me some presents to bring. There might even be one for you."

Rupert buried his nose in her hair. "Then I stand corrected."

"By the way, before I forget, Lady Marlborough said that your grandmother had loaned her son some money. Do you know anything about that?"

His mouth shrugged. "No, but it doesn't surprise me."

"She also mentioned that he had facilitated entrance to a royal event for your grandmother and was forgiven the loan as a consequence. Did she have a habit of manipulating people?"

"Now, hang on, Dodo. Just because she did something kind for someone and they return the favor does not make her a schemer." He would have sat up and made a show of indignation, but she could tell he was simply too tired. She felt the same. She must get some sleep soon.

"No offense intended," she murmured. "It's just that her generosity seems to have come with strings attached. It appears that she asked the vicar to perform some task and promised him the church would be a large beneficiary in her will— large enough to fix the church roof and put more electricity in the place."

This news surprised Rupert enough that he moved Dodo off his shoulder and sat up. "That *is* odd." His hair was sticking up in little tufts and she had to stifle a giggle. He looked adorable.

"And I assume you know that she had promised your Aunt Ruby the majority of her money."

He sat up straighter. "I did not! In fact, Grandmother was always talking about how irresponsible Uncle Lawrence was with money and that she would never waste her own on him."

"The web gets more and more tangled," Dodo said.

Rupert fell back against the sofa, the fit of righteous indignation apparently over. "I know that Granny was no saint, but I am surprised she would mislead people like that."

"But did she? You said yourself she was always calling her solicitor to change some small thing in her will. Perhaps you are wrong, and she did just as she said she would for all these people at one point in time, but then changed her will without telling them."

Rupert no longer had the energy to argue the point. The room was empty as each person must have gone upstairs after their interview.

55

"I'm off to bed," he said. "I can no longer put two sensible words together."

"Me too. My eyes are so heavy I can barely keep them open." They helped each other up the stairs.

"I'm sorry I'm so touchy," he said. "It's because it involves my family. Like when Bea was accused of murder in London."

"No offense taken. I totally understand. I would be the same if it were my family." She smiled.

"You never cease to amaze me, Dodo. Just when I deserve a rollicking, you offer forgiveness." He leaned in and left the merest whisper of a kiss that set her lips tingling and her heart wishing for more. "Goodnight, my darling."

"Goodnight."

Dodo woke around noon. Confused at first, she forgot that it was Christmas Day. Once she had her bearings, she remembered that she had some gifts to open. Looking around she saw that Lizzie had placed them on a chair. Upon opening the one from her parents, she squealed with delight at the bracelet laying on the ivory satin. It was a triple strand of pearls secured with a diamond clasp. Her mother may not be the most fashion-conscious woman in the world, but no one could fault her taste in jewelry.

Didi had given her a stylish, silk headscarf and a photo of the pair of them, in a solid silver frame. She hugged it to herself and felt the impulse to call and wish them a merry Christmas. They would be in the middle of a raucous game of charades right about now.

"Didi! Merry Christmas!"

"Dodo, how is Leicestershire?"

"Cold. We're having a white Christmas. I had a smashing time riding on a horse-drawn sleigh and tobogganing, yesterday. How about you?"

"Just rain down here. It's pretty gray."

"Too bad! How was Christmas Eve? Did Granny behave?"

"Not likely! She drew out the notes at the end of every carol at church so that hers was the only voice still singing."

"Just like her." Dodo chuckled.

"It's not the same without you, Dodo."

"I miss you too. Thank you for the lovely scarf and picture. It gave me a twinge of homesickness. What are the plans today?"

"The usual…with a twist," said Didi mysteriously.

"Now you have my attention."

There was a pause at the other end of the line. "What?" Dodo prodded.

"I should have told you, run it by you but…you have been so busy with Rupert and everything."

A pang of guilt shot through her. Didi was right, she had neglected her sister. She started drumming her nails on the telephone table. "Now you're making me nervous."

"Oh no! It's something good. At least, I hope you think it's good." Dodo could almost see her sister's golden curls bouncing but Didi's jitters were beginning to make her fidgety. "Out with it!"

"Charlie is coming to dinner."

"Charlie?"

Dodo and Charlie Chadworth had been an item several months before she met Rupert, but though Charlie had deep feelings for her, she could not reciprocate them.

Didi continued with excitement in her voice. "We met at a party some weeks ago and…well, we've been seeing each other most days." Her voice was still hesitant.

"That is simply marvelous!" cried Dodo. "I still feel bad about the way things ended with him, and you are the perfect cure! I'm truly delighted, little sister. You deserve one another. Such a lovely man."

"You don't know how relieved I am to hear that. I really like him, Dodo."

"Smashing! You make a perfect couple. I'm tickled pink."

"What about you? How's it going with Rupert's family?"

Now it was her turn to hesitate. "His father is welcoming but a little distant. As for his mother, she has the knives out for me, I think."

"Why on earth would she be like that? You've only just met her," cried Dodo.

"That's where things get a little tricky."

"Dodo…" Didi's tone held a note of warning.

"Rupert's grandmother died during Christmas Eve dinner. Fell right into her plate. It was awful."

"That *is* awful! Did it ruin Christmas?" asked Didi.

"You have no idea…she was murdered."

A strange sound came through the telephone.

"Didi?"

"I fell off the seat—literally. You are like a murder magnet."

"The thing is, if I hadn't been here the murderer would have got clean away with it. She was ninety-five and fragile and everyone but me assumed it was just her time. As a precaution, I leaned over the body and smelled cyanide. So, I had to alert the police."

"No wonder Rupert's mother isn't fond of you," Didi said with a laugh.

"It goes deeper than that."

Dodo explained about Etta Danforth's brother dying years before, when they were young, and how it had affected her.

"Tricky," agreed Didi. "Well, it sounds like you have your work cut out for you. Solve the crime and get back in her good books, I say."

"I hope it's that easy," she replied. "Look, don't tell Mummy. You know how she is."

"Of course. Do you want to talk to her?"

"Yes, please. And thanks again."

"When do I get to meet Rupert?"

"Soon, I promise."

"You had better make good on that! Now, hold on while I get them."

Didi went to get her parents and Dodo wished them a merry Christmas without mentioning the murder.

By the time she was done, Dodo had completely missed lunch, and tea wasn't for some time, so she headed through to the kitchen in search of a snack to tide her over, hopeful that it might give her the opportunity to talk to the staff.

Most stately homes housed the kitchens in the basement, but *Knightsbrooke Priory* was so old that the kitchens were in a former outbuilding, connected to the back of the main house several hundred years before, by a long corridor.

The kitchen was unexpectedly bright and modern with the latest in ovens and electric appliances. The Danforth's clearly valued their food. The place was bustling as they readied for the Christmas dinner but as she stepped in, a cloud of silence dropped over everyone. They stopped their work and stared.

"I do apologize," she began. "Please continue with your labors. I am just in search of a little snack."

The head cook stepped forward, a surprisingly thin, tall woman with a puff of graying hair. "What can I get for you, m'lady?" The rest of the staff went back to work.

"I missed lunch. Some bread and cheese would do the trick," she explained.

The woman's lips went tight with irritation and Dodo remembered too late, Lizzie's comment that she was rather severe.

Not the time to be asking questions.

"Of course, m'lady. If you will wait right here."

The cook sent a scullery maid into the oversized larder, and she returned with a chunk of Gloucester cheese and a crusty slice of bread.

Given the cook's cantankerous way, Dodo decided to take the food to her room.

Lizzie was there, and Dodo embellished the tale of asking for food until Lizzie was holding her sides in stitches. "She *is* an awfully serious person," said Lizzie. "There's very little talking at the servant's dinner—everyone is afraid of her."

"Well, I'm in the doghouse so I'll need you to find out if any of the staff saw anything unusual yesterday."

Lizzie twisted her mouth. "I'll do my best."

Dodo looked at the blue Tiffany box, her hands to her mouth.

"Take it," said Rupert, his mesmerizing eyes shining with excitement.

"You said Father Christmas wouldn't come," she said.

"I fibbed."

She opened the box and gasped. Winking up at her were two sapphire, teardrop, silver earrings. "Oh Rupert, they're perfect!" And she meant it.

She fiddled with her pearl studs and replaced them with the new jewels. "How do I look?"

In answer, he pulled her to him and kissed her. "I shall take that as a yes," she said with a laugh.

"Oh, and I almost forgot, Inspector Allingham is back in Father's study and would like a word with you."

She found the inspector installed behind the priceless desk.

"Lady Dorothea," he said in welcome. "Please take a seat." He laid down the pen he had been using and she leaned forward. "Did you learn anything of interest during the rest of the interviews?"

"They were pretty unsatisfactory as it happens. I didn't tell anyone my suspicions about her being murdered yet, so I had to frame my questions a little differently. Everyone believes it was just her time and no one mentioned being promised money. I was hoping something someone mentioned might tip me off, but no luck. I shall have to interview them again after I break the bad news."

"When do you plan to do that, Inspector?"

He picked up the pen again. "When everyone is gathered for tea. They've had time to calm down since witnessing Adelaide die, and I need to get a move on. Now that I can positively confirm the faint odor of bitter almonds on the napkin you used, coupled with the shocking redness of her skin, I can explain that both factors indicate poisoning by cyanide." He pulled the lid of the pen on and off. "How about you? Did your maid find out anything else that might be of use?"

"Not yet. I thought I might attempt to ask questions of the staff myself, but my efforts were thwarted. That cook is quite intimidating! I'll leave it all to Lizzie and pass to you what she learns." Her fingers played with the new earrings. "But I *can* tell you that Rupert had no idea that his grandmother had been promising people money in her will."

"Perhaps we should get a court order to look at it immediately instead of waiting until after the funeral," suggested the inspector. "I suspect it might be a significant clue. I'll use the telephone and see if I can convince a local magistrate to authorize one, now that we have validated that the deceased was murdered—but given that it's Christmas Day, I don't think it will happen until tomorrow."

"This has messed up your own Christmas plans hasn't it, Inspector?" she asked.

The cordial policeman sucked in his flabby cheeks. "Not really. I live alone and my parents are gone. I try to keep busy at this time of year. This fits the bill nicely."

Dodo felt a rush of compassion for him. "I shall see if my maid can get you a plate from our Christmas dinner and bring it in here for you."

The inspector leaned back in his chair, his hard features softening. "Well, that would be right nice of you, m'lady. I shan't turn that offer down."

Tea was already being served when she entered the drawing room and as promised, a few minutes later the inspector appeared. Every eye in the room was on him.

He cleared his throat and spoke in a calm, measured voice. "I want to thank everyone for their cooperation at this difficult time, but I am sorry to have to inform you that from the evidence gathered, I have concluded that Adelaide Danforth was murdered."

Gasps filled the room.

"How can that be?" cried Etta, shaking her head, her hands covering a face that was etched with anxiety.

"My mother was extremely old, Inspector. Are you absolutely sure?" asked Rupert's father, his palms spread wide.

"I am afraid there is no question, sir. All indicators point to death by cyanide poisoning."

The atmosphere that had been heavy-hearted, pivoted to alarm and Etta launched a glare laced with accusation at Dodo who had to look away.

Chapter 8

The inspector's announcement had effectively punctured any hope of salvaging Christmas. Dodo could not fault him for his delivery of the bad news; it had been understated and without drama. However, she had watched as the participants experienced a plethora of emotions they were ill-equipped to handle. Julia had sobbed and Beatrice's face had crumpled in distress. Most people left to seek isolation in their rooms until dinner.

As they now sat around the table, festivity seemed ill placed. Everyone wore a somber expression. Mrs. Danforth was particularly morose, hardly hiding a contempt for Dodo that seemed to be growing by the minute.

On the other hand, the food was exceptional, but it was hard to enjoy it in such a barbed atmosphere. The bright and jolly Christmas crackers lay untouched by the sides of their plates, hiding their treasures, and no one suggested pulling them.

Rupert endeavored to jump-start some kind of conversation, but after three failed attempts he abandoned the experiment. With their murdered grandmother lying in state upstairs, it just wasn't going to happen.

Everyone was at the meal except the vicar who had pastoral duties to perform throughout the day, and Lady Marlborough who had begged to be excused and had kept to her room.

When the butler finally brought in the flaming Christmas pudding, spirits rose briefly, but subsided along with the flames. Dodo was impatient to leave the awkwardness, even if the brandy sauce was arguably the best she had ever tasted.

As they sat in quiet groups in the drawing room, the rotund inspector entered again, and everyone held their breath. He glowed with satisfaction and Dodo was sure he was the only one who had really enjoyed the magnificent feast.

All heads rotated in his direction and Inspector Allingham cleared his throat.

"I have come to notify you that I have now opened an official inquiry into the murder of Mrs. Adelaide Danforth." He repositioned his tie which was now sitting at an odd angle. "Now that you have had time to process what happened and view the events of last night in a new light, if anyone has any information they think might move the case forward, I will be in Mr. Danforth's study for the next hour." As he looked at Dodo his eyes widened fractionally.

He moved toward the door. "I can also advise you that I have been successful in petitioning for an immediate reading of the will since the deceased was an exceptionally wealthy woman and there is some question as to who the major beneficiary is. The solicitor is on his way."

Dodo quickly scanned the faces to gauge the reactions to this revelation. Ruby and Lawrence looked at each other with concern but everyone else's features registered resignation.

"Hello, all!" said the vicar as he breezed in. Belatedly noticing the inspector addressing the group, he mumbled an apology.

"Oh, Reverend," said Beatrice. "The inspector says Granny was murdered!" He rushed to her side, placing an arm around her shoulder. "They are going to read Granny's will soon."

Rupert's mother shelved her disdain for Dodo long enough to share a worried glance with her husband. The vicar's face registered astonishment, swiftly followed by an expression that could only be described as triumphant.

"I shall be in the study." The inspector withdrew like an undertaker might, bowing and walking backward, which was rather fitting given the circumstances.

As soon as he left, a low hum began as people began talking to their neighbors.

"You think there will be some disappointed expectations, don't you?" whispered Rupert.

"I shall be watching everyone very closely when the contents of the document are read. I shall need your help as well as I can't possibly watch everyone at once."

"Are you sure? I thought I was suspect number one," he said, with a villainous grin. Dodo punched him on the arm.

Beatrice was still talking at length to the vicar who was consoling her, when Julia ran from the room. Dodo seized her departure as the perfect opportunity to follow her and offer a bit of sisterly advice. It would also provide her with a chance to visit the inspector without raising any eyebrows.

"I'll be back," she assured Rupert.

Dodo caught up with Julia in the cool hallway to the kitchens, noticing that the bandage on her wrist was absent. For half a second, she fantasized about hot radiators then reprimanded herself for a lack of focus. Julia was slumped on a bench, her head sagging to her chest and wiping large tears from her youthful face.

"Julia," she said gently.

The girl looked up with red-rimmed eyes and brushed at the tears harshly.

Dodo sat next to her. "Unrequited love is a bitter fruit, isn't it?"

"Is it that obvious?" she sobbed.

"Only to me." She was glad she wasn't Pinocchio and placed an arm around the young girl's shoulders.

"I know he's miles too old for me and I'm an utter frump, but he's the first handsome man to pay any attention to me." She looked up through watery eyes. "I think I love him."

She allowed Dodo to embrace her while she wept.

After several minutes, Dodo risked conversation and told her about Alexander Harrison, the son of a Viscount who was ten years her senior, who had snubbed her when she was fourteen. She had been mortified and was further shamed when she accidentally overheard him laughing about her with his friends.

Julia's face creased with incredulity. "You've had this happen too? I can't believe it! Look at you. You're stunning and sophisticated. It's obvious that Rupie is mad about you."

"It wasn't always this way," Dodo explained. "Unlike my sister, Didi, who was always pretty, I went through a terrible ugly duckling stage."

Julia lifted her head and dried her tears. "Honestly? You're not just being kind?"

Dodo put her hand over her heart. "Honestly."

"It is just so painful to see that he prefers Beatrice, and she hasn't even tried."

"How about when this"—Dodo waved her hand vaguely in the air—"is all over, I take you into London for a shopping trip with a visit to a beauty parlor?"

"Would you?" A desperate spark entered Julia's eyes.

Dodo brushed a tear away from Julia's cheek. "Of course! But first we will have to check with your mother." *And I'm not very popular with her.*

"Oh," Julia said, her face falling. "After Beatrice's problems…" She looked askance. "Mother is reluctant to let me out of her sight."

Dodo tapped her chin. "How persuasive is your brother?"

A modest smile crept onto Julia's lips. "Mother has a soft spot for Rupert and with all that he has done for Bea I believe he has earned some credits with her."

"Then let's have *him* ask her," declared Dodo, clapping her hands together.

Julia hugged herself. "I think I can bear all this heartache if I have something grown up and wonderful to look forward to." She sighed.

"Good! And take this from someone who knows, I would wager you only fancy yourself in love with Reverend Valentine because he is the lone, decent looking, single man under fifty this side of Coventry. When I saw Alexander years later, *he* was the one interested in *me*, and I was surprised to discover he had a big nose, prominent ears, and a weak chin. We tend to see through rose-colored glasses when we think ourselves in love."

"I'm not sure if I believe you," said Julia, twisting her lips. "But I will try to get over him."

"Good girl! Now you had better go upstairs and wash your face."

Dodo watched her run up the wide stairs and made for the study.

"Lady Dorothea, how good of you to come," said the inspector.

Dodo bit back a smile at the image of him inviting her to tea rather than to discuss the murder. "I gather you have something to tell me," she said.

"I just wanted to let you know that I have some people researching the incident with Mrs. Danforth's brother. Her maiden name was Forsythe."

Dodo touched her fingers to her brow. "I completely forgot to ask Rupert."

"Never mind, I asked her during the initial interview. I don't mind telling you she was on edge and obviously distraught by unwelcome memories, so she did not seem to think it odd that I asked." He stood the pen he was holding on its head. "I had a Dicken's of a time getting that court order for the will on Christmas Day, but I was insistent as I believe it will answer some of our questions and might cause the murderer to make a mistake if they are disappointed by its contents."

"Their body language might betray them," agreed Dodo. She looked at her watch. "Is that all? I'd better get back."

When she returned, she told Rupert that his youngest sister was lovesick and had gone to freshen up. He wrinkled his nose. "In love with the vicar? I don't know what they both see in him. My parents would never approve anyway. They have much higher aspirations for the pair of them."

"He's youngish, and he is available," explained Dodo. "Young girls are desperate for romance. It's just a crush for Julia. She'll get over it." She told him about her plans to take her to London. "I shall need your help to convince your mother to let her go since I'm still persona non grata."

"Of course." He took her hand and turned it over. "Mother is overwrought. She has several bouts of depression each year. Don't take it personally. I'm sure that given time she will warm up to you."

"Let's hope so."

The feeble looking solicitor was in his late seventies, his frame a little bent from pouring over documents for a living. Rupert guided him into the room and placed him at the small writing desk he'd had brought in. The group, which now included the vicar and Lady Marlborough, quietly waited as the solicitor withdrew gold rimmed spectacles from a battered leather case.

The lawyer peered at the faces in the room as though seeing them for the first time, then cleared his throat.

"The last will and testament of Adelaide Arundel Danforth." He paused, squinting and ran slowly through the legal language of preamble. "The bulk of my estate I leave to…" the infuriating man lifted his eyes from the paper again. "Rupert Fitzwilliam Danforth III—"

Fitzwilliam?

Hushed whispers of disbelief came from various quarters as Dodo scanned the room. Abject dejection was evident on the faces of both Rupert's aunt and uncle, and a query was stamped on the vicar's features. Lady Marlborough's face was as blank as a new sheet of paper.

The solicitor continued, his shaky voice a little raised "—my oldest grandson through the paternal line. To my faithful maid, Eliza, I leave two hundred pounds per annum until her death should she outlive me, and to my cook, Mrs. Howard, five hundred pounds for her retirement." He looked up. "Neither of these women survived the deceased."

The legal man adjusted his glasses and the knot of his black tie. Dodo sensed that he was nervous to continue.

"There is a codicil dated six months ago."

Hope stretched its wings in the faces of the Quintrells.

"To my daughter Ruby and her"—he coughed—"worthless husband Lawrence. Having demonstrated that you cannot be trusted to invest money wisely, I withhold mine from a similar fate."

Lawrence's face turned beet red.

"How could Mother be so cruel?" gasped Ruby.

"Ahem."

The Quintrells were shamed into silence.

"To the new vicar, Dante Valentine, I thank him for firing the choir director as I requested but if he believes I would waste my wealth on a tumbledown church roof, his faith is truly misplaced.

Let the parishioners raise the funds themselves. It will be more appreciated that way."

The Reverend Valentine's face drained of color as every eye in the room flashed to him.

"I...I...ummm..." he stuttered, fingering the dog collar at his neck.

The solicitor cleared his throat. He was not done. "To my dearest friend Millicent Marlborough. Our children do not often reflect their parents' values, and such is the case with your boy, William. He was a useful tool when I wanted to attend the Queen's garden party and I paid him handsomely for the favor at the time. I think you will agree that my duty to him is done."

Lady Marlborough's face did not move, though her lips tightened forming a frame of deep lines.

"There are small bequests to servants and friends, but I won't bore you with those details," continued the solicitor. "And I feel it only proper to add that Mrs. Adelaide Danforth had made an appointment with me for January second, eight days hence." The low light showed beads of sweat on the man's furrowed upper lip as he rolled the will into a scroll and handed it to Rupert.

"Unless you need me for anything else, I shall get back to my family," he said to Rupert's father.

"Was my mother of sound mind when she wrote this codicil?" demanded Ruby before he could leave.

"I have rarely met a more lucid nonagenarian than your mother," said the solicitor, donning his hat and making for the door. He glanced at Rupert. "I trust I can sort out the details with you after Christmas? Goodbye."

The vicar looked like a mouse at a cat convention. "I must go too. I interrupted my visits to the poor to attend." He shot from the room on the solicitor's tails.

Ruby and Lawrence were only just holding it together and soon left the room with the excuse that Ruby had a headache.

Inspector Allingham had clearly found the whole event rather entertaining and was failing to hide a smile.

If someone had killed Adelaide before she changed her will, the blood on their hands had been wasted.

Chapter 9

Everyone else disappeared and Dodo and Rupert were left alone with Inspector Allingham.

"It seems I owe you an apology," said Rupert under his breath.

"Well, that was a rum thing," exclaimed the inspector as he walked toward them. "A lot of disappointed and upset people. Was she always like that, your granny?"

Rupert huffed. "She was a rock in my life and always nice to me, but I don't deny she had a dark side."

"I'd say we saw that today." The inspector chuckled into his bristly mustache.

Rupert turned to Dodo. "You thought she manipulated people with the promise of money, and it turns out you were spot on."

"No one likes to think ill of their grandmother, and it doesn't mean she didn't have other admirable qualities," said Dodo.

"It appears in this instance, though, it was a misplaced defense," he said.

"Water under the bridge."

"Did you pick up on anything from people's reactions?" asked the inspector.

"Rupert's aunt and uncle were caught completely unaware by the personal slight, and the discovery that they were cut out. I imagine their finances are at critical level," she said. "Might be worth looking into. The vicar was mortified—couldn't wait to get out of here. It is humiliating to think you have ingratiated yourself, especially when one is a vicar. Love of mammon and all that."

"What about Lady Marlborough?" asked the inspector.

"Having one of her dearest friends ridicule her offspring is never going to go down well," remarked Dodo. "But she could not have known about it before so it cannot be considered a motive."

The inspector looked at Rupert. "You didn't seem surprised, sir, if I might say so."

"Knowing what I know now, perhaps I should have been!" Rupert shrugged. "But Father has the inheritance from his father, and it was just understood that Grandmother would want to keep the fortune together and pass it down to her son's son."

The inspector smoothed his hair which had a copious amount of brilliantine in it. "Has your maid found anything interesting, Lady Dorothea?"

"I haven't talked to her about it yet. Shall I send for her?" asked Dodo.

"If you wouldn't mind," replied Inspector Allingham. "I want to know where the murderer got the cyanide from. Most country houses use it to keep vermin at bay, so the servants may be talking about it. Of course, the killer could have brought it with them, which means I will have to dig through the bins." He shook his head. "Usually, that's the job of the constables but we are short staffed for Christmas. But I'd like to know if there is any available in the house or garden sheds before I get this suit dirty."

When Lizzie appeared, Dodo could tell from the glint in her eye that she had something interesting to share.

"Ah, Miss Perkins," said the inspector. "I understand from Lady Dorothea that you have been looking into things in the servant's quarters." He laid a heavy emphasis on the last two words. "Do you have anything to tell us?"

Lizzie clasped her hands. "I can tell you that no strangers came to the house while the family were at the church, at least none that anyone saw. But I have also learned that the cook keeps potassium cyanide crystals at the back of the big larder to use in the case of rats. It's been there for at least ten years, and they haven't used it in five since there is a mouser cat who does a good job. But the minute she heard that the old lady was poisoned with cyanide, the cook got all dizzy and had to sit in a chair fanning herself."

"Did she send anyone to check it?"

"Oh yes! She immediately sent Nancy, one of the scullery maids, to get it. The housekeeper took it from her. She handled it very carefully with a handkerchief and said it had been years since she'd needed it and then held it up to the light. The lid was slightly crooked, and she could tell from smudges in the dust that it had been opened recently."

"Is that so?" said the inspector.

"They were ready to come and tell you when you sent for me."

The wry grin on his face made Dodo think he was probably thanking heaven he would not need to search through the rubbish bins.

"I shall take it for fingerprints." He rubbed his nose. "Do you think any of the servants had anything against Adelaide Danforth?"

"Playing on the fact that I am a stranger here, I asked about the older Mrs. Danforth," replied Lizzie. "Most of the kitchen staff had nothing but kind words to say about her. Same with the footmen. But the lady's maid who attends her, Doreen, was quiet so I chatted with her alone during tea. The old lady's own maid passed away several years ago and rather than hire another, Doreen saw to both the ladies. She was very respectful in her words, but I could tell she was holding something back. But she doesn't know me so that's to be expected. I asked Betty, one of the parlor maids about it. She was only too happy to tell me that—" She flicked her eyes to Rupert and paused.

"It's fine Lizzie," he assured her. "I want to find out who did this to Granny as much as anyone. Tell us everything you know."

"Well, she said that the old lady led Doreen a merry dance at times but that recently she had made life particularly awkward for Doreen by asking her to do things that weren't quite… proper."

"Like what?" asked Dodo.

"She wouldn't be specific, but she did say that the old lady promised to name Doreen in her will if she did those things for her."

Rupert bit his cheek. "How devious Granny was. I had no idea. I wonder if my parents knew?"

"If you could ask them that would be very helpful," said the inspector. "They certainly did not disclose anything of that nature to me in their interviews but that was before they knew we were dealing with a murder and before we knew the contents of the will and the promises that had been made."

"Will do," said Rupert.

"That's another person disappointed by the actual wording of the will. Doreen," Dodo pointed out. "A servant would certainly be excited by the prospect of any money—it might mean they could retire."

"I shall need to interview this Dora," said the inspector.

"Doreen," corrected Lizzie. "And there's more. Lady Marlborough's lady's maid, Warren, was very withdrawn which is not out of character, but I tried to make small talk with her about the poison. She wasn't having any of it. Excused herself and went to her room."

The inspector added the name of Warren to his notebook. "Perhaps she saw something that has made her uneasy. Right, I shall come and talk to them within the hour. Can you let them know, Miss Perkins?"

"Of course." Lizzie left the room.

"What a corker!" exclaimed the inspector. "Excellent investigator. Now, there's a lot of things to process from what she has told us." The inspector began to check his notes. "We have a wealthy widow who we know had promised several people money after she died who talked of meeting with her solicitor to change her will. Anyone she had made that promise to must be listed as a suspect."

"I agree," said Dodo. "And the fact that the cyanide may have come from the house tilts the evidence toward a less premeditated crime. It points toward someone hearing something while they were here that propelled them to take hasty action."

The inspector moved to the door. "I need to collect that cyanide tin from the kitchen before it gets even more contaminated." He stopped with his hand on the door handle and directed a question to Rupert. "Who was present when your grandmother talked about changing her will while she was asleep?"

"The immediate family and Dodo. My aunt and uncle had not yet arrived."

"Nor had Lady Marlborough," Dodo reminded him. "But it does not seem that Adelaide was timid about broadcasting her intentions. She could have mentioned it several times to people, and we wouldn't know."

"Let's say she did," said Rupert, "and one of them decided to take action to prevent her doing that. How long does cyanide take to work?"

"It varies, depending on different factors," explained the inspector. "Amount administered, weight of the target, whether the target has eaten."

"But are we talking minutes, seconds, hours?" asked Rupert.

"It is not as fast acting as most people think. It can take up to fifteen minutes," said Dodo. "But we do not believe it was in her food or her wine glass, so we have no idea when she ingested it."

The inspector gripped his chin in thought. "Let's hope the tin holds some answers—"

A blood curdling scream interrupted him.

Chapter 10

"What the—" cried the inspector as he ran from the room, Dodo and Rupert following in his wake.

Lady Marlborough was leaning over the banister, wailing and waving a handkerchief in the direction of her room, gasping for breath through her cries.

The middle-aged inspector bounded up the stairs two at a time and rushed into Lady Marlborough's room. When Dodo caught up, she saw the feet of someone on the floor and the inspector leaning over them.

Her stomach dropped.

"She's gone," declared the inspector as he pulled back on his haunches.

"Who?" asked Dodo

"Warren, Lady Marlborough's maid."

"No!"

Dodo took a step forward and could see that the maid's arms were bent under her in an unnatural manner and her scarlet face was strained. Upon further inspection she noticed deep lines around the eyes and mouth, a mouth that bore signs of white foam.

"She's still warm, so it has only recently happened," he announced. "Looks like cyanide poisoning again."

"What the devil!" cried Rupert who was hovering by the door, keeping an eye on the hysterical Lady Marlborough. "Why would anyone kill the maid?"

Lady Marlborough staggered into the room, clutching the door frame. "I never thought she would go through with it," she wailed.

The inspector snapped his head toward her. "Go through with it?" he asked. "Can you explain?"

Rupert led Lady Marlborough to a chair in her room. She sat, wiping her eyes and nose and lifted a face carved with sorrow.

"She had been depressed for some time," she began. "I thought it was a storm in a teacup, but I suppose I was wrong."

"Do you know what she was depressed about?" asked the inspector.

Her loose mouth shrugged. "The usual I would say. Realizing that life was passing her by and that sort of thing. She recently had her fiftieth birthday and comprehended that her hopes of marrying and having a family were never going to come to pass. I thought a change of venue might help and agreed to come here for Christmas. It can be a hard time for some people. Ohhhh!" She wailed again and Dodo patted her shoulder.

"Whatever is the matter?" asked Mrs. Danforth, appearing in the doorway. Her frenzied eyes darted from Lady Marlborough to Rupert then to Dodo, finally catching on the legs of the figure on the floor. Her agonized glare fell back to Dodo with buckets of reproach.

The week was turning out to be an unmitigated disaster.

Rupert went to his mother. "Let's go to your room and you can have a lay down. I'll get someone to bring you some tea."

"What happened?" she whimpered. "Is it another murder?" Her tone was pleading for Rupert to tell her that it was an accident.

"At the moment we are leaning toward suicide." He wrapped his arm around his mother's shoulder and walked her down the corridor.

The inspector snapped his attention back to Lady Marlborough. "Walk me through recent events, m'lady. How did you come to find her here?"

"I could see that everyone was disappointed by the will, myself included to be honest. Titles are one thing, but money is quite another and our estate needs significant repairs that will cost far more than our means will allow. However, I felt like an interloper in a moment of familial distress and was desperate to leave the tension of the room. I wandered around the halls for a good while, looking out at the snowy landscape and realized I was chilled to the bone, so I came upstairs to find a coat to wear."

She ran a hand across her forehead to sweep back some strands of hair that had fallen in her agitation. "I didn't see

Warren at first and I walked over to the wardrobe and pulled out a wrap. It wasn't until I turned…" Her lips quivered. "There she was. It was terrible."

A blue, cape-like wrap lay over the end of the bed.

"Did you find a suicide note?" asked the inspector as he stood.

A palm went to her chest. "I didn't think to look, I could think of nothing but flight."

The inspector commenced a careful inspection of the floor and under the bed, the bedside tables and the rest of the carpet and furniture.

"Nothing here. I shall go to her room. Everyone thinks cyanide kills instantly so perhaps she was surprised that it hadn't worked and left her room." He dusted off his knees. "Lady Dorothea, would you stay here with Lady Marlborough while I go and check the maid's room?"

"Of course."

When they were left alone, Dodo rang the bell. She did not trust the water in the pitcher by the bed. A thought crashed through her brain. Could Lady Marlborough have been the intended victim? This was a much more likely scenario.

She placed the wrap over the body so that Lady Marlborough was not forced to stare at it.

"Is there someone I can call for you?" she asked the flustered, trembling woman.

"That is very kind of you," Lady Marlborough replied. "If someone could contact my son, William. He is all I need." She leaned over to the handbag by her feet and popped open the clasp. With blue-veined hands she withdrew a small notebook and a pencil with a tassel on the end. Another paper slipped from the notebook, which she crushed and dropped back into the bag.

She ripped out the first page that had been used and began to scribble a number.

"Here!" She carefully tore the page out, handing it to Dodo. "Please tell him to come and get me as soon as possible. I came on the train but that will be impossible without a maid…" Her pale eyes searched Dodo's face for understanding.

Dodo doubted very much that the inspector would let Lady Marlborough leave anytime soon but decided against mentioning it.

Instead, she asked, "Shall I help you down the stairs?" wondering how she would manage to take the heavyset woman down alone.

"I have no fear of the dead," she warbled. "It was just such a shock finding her." Her gnarled hands were clasped under her nose as if in fervent prayer.

Dodo was almost positive the inspector would want Lady Marlborough out of the room in order to make a thorough search, but a few more minutes to recover from the shock wouldn't hurt.

"Then I hope you understand that I shall have to wait until the inspector returns," Dodo explained. "It's protocol."

"Ah," nodded the old woman, her large brows knitted together.

A knock on the door indicated the arrival of a parlor maid and Dodo asked for two cups of tea, no tray.

Dodo was used to dead bodies, but to have to exist in the same space as one brought a new level of awkwardness. And then there was the nagging reality that her ladyship had probably defied death. If that was the case, the killer would likely try again. They would need to provide her with security.

Dodo forced herself to smile and decided small talk might help. "How long was your maid with you?"

"Seven years."

"That is quite a long time for a lady's maid in this day and age, is it not?"

"Is it? I don't think so. My friends have had theirs for much longer. My mother's maid died in her service." She sniffed. "The maid I had before Warren married. She was sixty and had been with me for twenty years. She met someone at an hotel we stayed at." Her face became hard. "I regret it to this day."

"Surely not," protested Dodo. "You cannot begrudge someone their happiness. Especially those who put our interests above their own."

The gray, wiry eyebrows crinkled like two elderly caterpillars. "She had promised she would never leave me. I can't abide broken promises. Warren was never as good. Never, God rest her soul."

This line of conversation had clearly been a mistake. It was time to leave the touchy subject.

"How far away is your son?" she asked.

"Oh, he lives in the manor in Warwickshire. It's about a two-hour drive. Longer on the train."

"And is he married?"

Her countenance brightened at mention of her son. "Oh, yes. He has given me three grandchildren who are grown themselves now. They are all married, and I have six great-grandchildren." Her gaze became unfocused.

And yet you would deny such happiness to the serving class.

Dodo glanced back at the body. She was itching to have a nose around but thought it indelicate in the circumstances.

Rupert put a nose in the door. "Goodness, Mumsy is rather shaken." He glanced at Lady Marlborough. "How are you faring?"

"I'm feeling better now, my heart has stopped racing. Where is that tea?"

The door stood ajar, and the inspector popped in, his face flushed.

"Nothing there."

The maid reappeared with two cups of tea looking flustered at seeing four people in the room.

"Here!" said Dodo reaching out her hands. She gave one cup to Lady Marlborough and took a long sip of her own before sidling over to the inspector and telling him of her fears for Lady Marlborough.

His eyes crinkled in thought. "I believe you are right, Lady Dorothea."

"I should test the water in the jug and tumbler and put Lady Marlborough under police guard, if I were you."

The inspector coughed. "I was about to suggest the same thing."

Another maid came into the room. "If you please, there are some people here to see the inspector."

"That will be the fingerprint people," he explained. "Alrighty, I need everyone out of this room, please. Yourself included your ladyship. Until we find out otherwise, I am treating this as another murder. Now, if you will excuse me."

"I was rather hoping it was the undertaker," whispered Rupert. "Having two dead bodies in the house is completely undoing Mother."

He helped Lady Marlborough out of her chair and handed her the cane.

"I am still rather cold and feeling the effects of the shock," she said. "Please take me to the drawing room while your young lady calls my son."

It took some time to descend the stairs with Lady Marlborough clutching the railing and Rupert's arm as she slowly took each step. Dodo held the cane. Once she was installed with a lap blanket next to the fire, Dodo went to the telephone.

When she was put through, she said, "Hello! Lord Marlborough? My name is Lady Dorothea Dorchester, and I am a member of a house party that includes your mother."

"Lady who?" he barked.

"Lady Dorothea Dorchester. Look, there have been a couple of tragedies involving her old friend Adelaide Danforth and your mother's maid."

"Something up with Mater, you say?"

"Yes! Lady Marlborough is in need of some support but is unable to leave. Would you be able to come to *Knightsbrooke Priory*?"

"Come? But it's Christmas Day! Can't it wait until tomorrow?" His voice was a cross between a seal and a camel.

"Perhaps I wasn't clear," Dodo almost shouted. "Your mother's friend and her maid have been *murdered*, Lord Marlborough, and we are not sure that your mother was not the intended target."

"Oh well, if you put it like that." His bad humor leaked through the line. "I shall send someone to bring her home."

Dodo clenched her jaw. "I apologize for not explaining the situation more explicitly. The police have not given permission for anyone to leave the premises and your mother needs

79

consolation from her family. Her nerves are very fragile at the moment, and she asked for you specifically."

Dodo heard the sound of a deep sigh of exasperation. "Is she in danger? If she is, I demand that she be able to come home."

"The police are here and will place a guard outside her room. You really should come yourself."

"If you insist," he finally said. "I shall be there as soon as I can but with this weather, I'm not sure when that will be."

With deep dissatisfaction, Dodo replaced the earpiece.

What a thoroughly obnoxious man!

Chapter 11

Dodo walked across to the kitchen in search of Lizzie whom she found consoling the staff. The news about Warren had traveled fast.

The usually bustling workspace was now devoid of activity. All culinary labors had ground to a halt. The surly cook who had been so stiff and annoyed at Dodo's request for bread and cheese such a short time ago, was now a shadow of her former austere self. Her straight, unyielding spine was curved into a hump, like a tree trunk battered over by a storm. Her gray head hung low over the empty table, her chapped hands clasping and unclasping.

"I feel right guilty about all this," she muttered. "Two deaths all because I have that stupid stuff in the pantry. If I could go back in time and remove it..." The cook's bony face collapsed, and she blew her nose like a foghorn into a large man's handkerchief.

"There, there," said Lizzie, patting the sharp shoulder of the cook. Two scullery maids, who were also at the table, looked like sad puppies, watching their tea get cold. The woeful atmosphere made Dodo shudder.

"Can I have a word?" said Dodo who was standing behind her maid.

Lizzie looked up with wide eyes. "I didn't see you there, m'lady. Of course." She pushed back from the table, the haunted eyes of the scullery maids following her.

"It's just dreadful!" Lizzie declared when they were alone. "They can't handle two deaths in less than twenty-four hours. I'm not sure I can! Warren was not the most pleasant of people, but I wouldn't wish this on her. Perhaps that is why she was so distant?"

"Perhaps." She nodded. "I'm having my own troubles. Rupert's mother blamed me for bringing a curse on the house after the first murder." Dodo crossed her arms. "You should have seen the filthy look she gave me when she found out about Warren's death."

"Fear makes people do odd things," said Lizzie.

"According to Rupert she's prone to mood swings and bouts of depression. If I could just clear these murders up quickly, it would go a long way to redeeming me, I think."

Lizzie's head snapped up. "Murders? We heard it was a suicide."

"Of the two options I prefer it to be suicide, but we can't be sure and there's no note. In my opinion it's more likely that the wrong person died."

"Good heavens!" exclaimed Lizzie. "You mean Lady Marlborough?"

A cool draft wrapped itself around Dodo's shoulders and she pulled her cardigan close.

"Would you say Warren's behavior rose to the level of being depressed or suicidal?"

Lizzie tutted. "Like I said, she was not what you might call a ray of sunshine. Always complaining about the cold—"

"Well, I am with her on that," declared Dodo.

"She was what my mum would call a right moaning Minnie, but now that she's dead it could have been because she was unhappy. I'm not sure she gave off the impression of being suicidal though." A pang of guilt flittered across Lizzie's face. "I gave her a wide berth if you must know. I can't abide negative people. And she put on airs and graces because her mistress had a title. She was less than polite to the housekeeper. There's no call for that. But while you were all at church, she withdrew into her shell even more and disappeared up to her room. Had all her food brought up to her on a tray. I didn't see her again before we heard she had offed herself. Perhaps I should have made more of an effort." The guilt returned, taking up residence behind her eyes.

"You couldn't have known, Lizzie, and if she rebuffed the rest of the staff…"

"She did. But still. A little Christian kindness might have made all the difference."

"Well, I'm not convinced it's suicide. It's too convenient. And if it was really meant for her ladyship, then Warren's death was accidental."

They had wandered out of the hallway by the kitchen and were back in the main house near the stairs. They both jumped as Inspector Allingham ran down waving his arms around.

"I found it," he cried in triumph. "A suicide note, in her pocket. She *did* kill herself."

Dodo frowned. "Really?"

Lady Marlborough was not *the intended target?*

The inspector shook his head. "Now that I've read her letter, it makes things clear." He paused, she supposed for dramatic tension. Never one to have an abundance of patience, Dodo gritted her teeth and stared at him.

"It's a confession!" he declared.

Dodo reared back in confusion. "A confession to murdering Adelaide Danforth?"

"Yes! She said she couldn't take the guilt and had to put an end to it."

"Why on earth would a visiting maid kill Adelaide? They didn't even know each other as far as I know," she said. "Did Warren give a reason?"

"No." The inspector dragged fingers down his mustache. "But she confessed, what more do you need?"

A cloak of skepticism draped itself over Dodo's shoulders.

"May I read it?" she asked.

"It's still in the room," said the inspector, his former enthusiasm waning. "And it will be dusted for prints. I can't let anyone else touch it."

"Of course," mumbled Dodo.

"But I can relate the details as it's very short. '*I killed Adelaide Danforth. The devil made me do it. I cannot live with the guilt. I have to end it all'*."

"Have you read many suicide notes, Inspector? Does it follow the pattern?" she asked.

"I have not as it happens. Only one other, but I did take a course in investigating suicides and it was suggested that such notes seem to be on the shorter side."

"It just seems odd that she mentions no motive. I would think a person who has killed another and confesses would want others to know why they did it," said Dodo. "Let's tell Lady Marlborough and ask her opinion. She knows her best."

"I was headed that way when I saw you," he said.

A young constable was outside the drawing room, and he nodded to his superior as they entered. Lady Marlborough's head was leaning against the side of the sofa her eyes closed. Inspector Allingham cleared his throat and the hawk like eyes dragged open.

"Yes?"

He told her about finding the confession.

"Does this fit with the person you know?" he asked her.

Lady Marlborough waved her handkerchief. "Nothing fits, Inspector. And I am not aware that my maid had ever met Adelaide before. But then, if she was mentally unstable nothing would make sense, would it?"

"Perhaps a look into Warren's previous life will determine whether it has ever intersected with Adelaide's," Dodo suggested. "I still cannot see that Warren would murder her without any motive. It makes no sense at all."

"Barking mad," muttered Lady Marlborough.

"Excuse me?" said the inspector as Dodo tried to hide a smile.

"Warren *was* depressed about her unmarried status. Perhaps it drove her mad."

They left Lady Marlborough by the fire and the inspector went back to his work, dejected by Dodo's lack of belief in the authenticity of the letter.

"Let's go up to my room so we can have a little think in private," suggested Dodo to Lizzie. "I need to talk things through."

"You're still not convinced?" Lizzie asked.

Dodo puffed air through her nose. "It feels wrong."

Her bedroom was still warm from the fire that had been stoked that morning and Dodo felt all her muscles relax as she sat in a velvet armchair by the hearth. Lizzie took its twin.

"For argument's sake, let's say Warren's death is a suicide."

"Alright," said Lizzie, waiting for the cogs to turn in her mistress's sharp mind.

"And let's consider the confession to be true," continued Dodo. "Why would she do it? And why would she not give her reason? Warren has no connection to this family as far as we know and according to Lady Marlborough. If it had been her ladyship's former maid, I might have been less suspicious as she would have met Adelaide, but in recent years, the two old ladies have seen very little of each other." She tapped her foot on the rug. "If Warren did cross paths with her, it would have to stem from her former life, before she became Lady Marlborough's maid. I shall suggest that the inspector look into her work history."

"The inspector will have the resources to do that, though it might take a bit longer with it being Christmas," said Lizzie.

Dodo's mind was busy arranging information into a pattern. "And why would Warren kill her even if they *had* met before?" She snapped her fingers. "We know Adelaide had a habit of promising wealth to manipulate people, perhaps she promised Warren money a long time ago? It seems rather a large coincidence."

"And you don't like coincidences," said Lizzie. "You think maybe she heard about Adelaide Danforth talking of changing her will?"

"That's the theory we were favoring before Warren died," said Dodo. "Can you remember if she said anything that might suggest she knew Rupert's grandmother?"

Lizzie smacked her head. "I have just remembered something. When Warren arrived and introduced herself, she said it was her first time here, so unless Mrs. Adelaide Danforth visited Lady Marlborough's home in the last seven years, I would say you are right, they had never met."

"Very good, Lizzie. Anything else?"

Lizzie shook her head.

An idea began to sprout. "I'm still not convinced. I don't suppose she wrote anything while she was here?" asked Dodo.

"Who, Warren? Probably. I make all sorts of lists of things you will need and give them to the housekeeper on arrival. Any

85

lady's maid would do the same." Lizzie pointed at Dodo. "You mean to compare the handwriting to the suicide note, don't you?"

"Bravo Lizzie! You're developing into a fine detective."

Lizzie's cheeks turned pink. "Thank you!" she said with a shy smile. "I'll ask the housekeeper."

"Now, I'd better find Rupert before I'm missed." She raised her palms to the warmth of the fire. "I give you permission to stay in here for as long as you want."

As she turned to leave, Lizzie put a hand on her arm. "Rupert's mother will come around," she said gently. "These murders have spoiled everything. You'll win her over in the end. You always do."

Dodo hugged her. "Thank you."

As she passed Lady Marlborough's room, she saw the fingerprint people hard at work.

She found Rupert in the large foyer petting the dogs. "Where have you been?" he asked. "I was going to send out a search party."

"Snooping and analyzing," she said quietly.

"Ah, I should have known."

"What are you doing here with the dogs?" she asked.

"Avoiding," he said with a grin. "The inspector informed everyone they would need to have their prints taken. It didn't go down too well. Lady Marlborough took it as a personal insult."

"I can well imagine," she said with a laugh. "I suppose that will include me too."

"I've had mine done." He lifted fingertips that still bore the remnants of black ink on them. "I'll walk with you."

Outside his father's study, they could hear Lady Marlborough brow-beating the inspector. The door blasted open, and they came face to face with the red-faced woman.

"It's just a formality so they can eliminate people," Dodo explained to her. "They will look for prints in your room, on the note, and so forth. Then they will compare them to all our prints."

"Well, my prints will be all over my blessed room," she puffed.

"That is true," said Dodo. "But police work is, of necessity, methodical."

86

Lady Marlborough stalked off, thrusting her cane hard into the ground and slowly pulling herself along. One foot seemed particularly weak.

"Can I help?" asked Rupert as they watched her painfully slow and arduous progress.

Lady Marlborough swung her cane up and waved it at him. "I am not an invalid, young man!" she wailed.

Rupert retreated and he and Dodo entered the study.

"Hello," said the inspector looking ruffled and hot. "That was a lot harder than it should have been!"

"I don't doubt it," Dodo responded. She held out her fingers for the ink pad. "My maid is going to try to find something with Warren's handwriting on it for comparison."

The inspector paused to consider before pressing her fingertips to a clean sheet of paper.

"You still think it's a forgery? I'm hoping it's not and I can be done with the case, but no one can ever say I'm not thorough. And that is a good idea if you can find a sample. It will clear the matter up once and for all."

Dodo rolled her inky fingers against the paper.

"I don't suppose you've had time to confirm the claim that your grandmother was asking Doreen to do suspect things, have you?" the inspector asked Rupert, checking that Dodo's prints had transferred acceptably to the paper.

"I did ask my parents and they were floored. Had no idea. Father wonders if some kind of dementia was beginning to set in."

"At her age that could certainly be the case."

"Have you been able to test the water and the glass?" Dodo asked the inspector, wiping her fingers with a wet towel.

"No cyanide present in either so she didn't consume the poison in that room, in my opinion."

"That's good and suggests that Lady Marlborough is not in any danger."

"The only person in danger is me from her wrath," the inspector chuckled.

When Dodo and Rupert returned to the rest of the family, Julia was saying, "I know I shouldn't say it when poor Granny has been murdered, but it is rather exciting being fingerprinted."

"Julia!" remonstrated her snappish mother. "Decorum is required."

This shut down the poor girl as effectively as a bucket of cold water to the head.

In contrast, despite the drama playing out in her home, Beatrice was looking better every day. Her thick hair had a healthy sheen, and her young skin was glowing.

The vicar came through the door soon after Dodo and Rupert. "I got a call that I should come to be fingerprinted," he remarked, blowing on his red hands.

Beatrice's countenance lit up at his arrival, endowing her face with a special sort of beauty. She held up her own blackened fingers for his inspection. "Oh, Dante! It's all rather ghastly."

Dodo was reminded that Beatrice had recently been fingerprinted in connection with another crime and that it might bring back difficult memories.

The Reverend Valentine hurried over to Beatrice like a fly to light, and Julia's face filled with thunder. But Dodo was pleased to see that instead of striding out of the room, she merely tossed her head.

Good girl!

As romantic tension buzzed around the room, Inspector Allingham entered. "My people are just finishing upstairs. Thank you for your patience."

Lady Marlborough muttered something under her breath and thumped her cane on the floor in protest.

"When is my son arriving?" she asked to the room in general.

Oops! I forgot to tell her.

"He had some things to attend to and said he would set off after that," Dodo replied. "But the weather may delay him."

"I can't wait to get home," Lady Marlborough muttered.

Inspector Allingham raised his hand. "No, no, no. I can't have anyone leave yet." He turned to Rupert's father. "Do you have another room we can move Lady Marlborough to?"

"Absolutely!" he responded, rubbing a palm over his shiny head. "One thing this old pile has is plenty of space. I'll get a girl to set a fire this instant."

"Then my son will need a room too," Lady Marlborough snarled.

"I'll take care of it," Mr. Danforth assured her as he and the inspector turned to leave.

Dodo followed Allingham out.

"Have you searched the maid's room again?" she asked.

"I have just come from there," he said.

"Anything odd?"

"No trace of the cyanide. I was hoping to find a container or bag that held the crystals, but nothing."

Lizzie appeared holding a piece of paper. She shook it. "A list written by Warren."

Inspector Allingham frowned.

"Lady's maids often write lists of things their mistresses might need," Dodo explained. "Do you have the suicide note?"

His hand went to his neck. "It's evidence. I had to leave it in the room. It's being dusted and will be used for comparison with the prints we've taken from the guests and family."

Dodo wanted answers. "Couldn't you take this up there for a handwriting comparison right now?"

The inspector's lower lip pushed out the bristles of his mustache. "I don't see why not. I'll be right back." He thundered up the stairs.

"The cook is still in a right state," Lizzie said. "She's in no position to make the dinner. The housekeeper has put her to bed and is directing the scullery maids. It could be a disaster."

"I'm sure we can survive on cold cuts for one meal," said Dodo. "It's a nasty business, and the cook must feel the burden of guilt, though she shouldn't."

The inspector was running back down the stairs, energy animating his bland features.

"It's not a match!" he declared.

"Are you sure?"

"I examined them carefully. It was close. Someone had taken great pains to copy her style but even my less than expert eye could tell that it was a forgery."

"Right!" said Dodo. "A fake suicide note confirms my theory that Warren was actually murdered, and someone is covering it up. It also validates that she did not die accidentally in place of her mistress. She was targeted. But it does beg the question as to why she needed to be silenced?"

"Who would have known what her handwriting looked like?" asked the inspector.

"Lady Marlborough, the kitchen staff as they gathered the things on the list, and anyone who went into the kitchen for any reason. It was out in the open for anyone to see," pointed out Lizzie. "The killer could have snatched anything she wrote to copy the style."

"It would also explain why there is no trace of the cyanide in her room," said Dodo. "She didn't kill Adelaide. But I would wager that she saw who did, or at least saw something that led her to know who it was. Lizzie, you said she was withdrawn while we were at the church. Perhaps she saw someone take the cyanide earlier and it made her uncomfortable. Then when Adelaide died, her conscience condemned her."

"Or maybe she tried to blackmail the murderer," suggested Lizzie.

"Oh Lizzie! Yes! We've seen how badly that works out, before."

"That would mean we are looking at one murderer," said the inspector. "And it's probably one of the people in there." He pointed to the door of the drawing room. "Though I still need to interview this Doreen. Right now, I want to get back and study the prints we got from the cyanide tin and the room. I'll let you know what I discover."

Lizzie went back to the servant's area and Dodo slipped back into the drawing room.

"It wasn't suicide," she whispered into Rupert's ear.

"No?" His loud exclamation attracted the attention of the other occupants. Dodo cringed. "Sorry," he said quietly. "How do you know?"

"Let's take the dogs for a walk," Dodo suggested.

When they were bundled up outside where no one could hear them, Dodo explained the latest discoveries.

"So, Granny's murderer needed to silence Warren for some reason."

"Exactly. My guess is that she either witnessed something she shouldn't or made a deduction and had to be eliminated."

"What a Christmas this is turning out to be!" he declared.

"So, it brings us back to the will, I think," said Dodo.

"That does seem most logical," Rupert agreed.

"This conclusion implicates your aunt and uncle, the vicar, Doreen and who knows how many others?"

She pulled down the snug woolen hat over her ears.

"You look wiped out," he said, running a finger along her chin that sent a tickling sensation weaving through her. "You should make it an early night and start with a fresh slate tomorrow."

She glanced at her watch. A low-grade headache was banging around her head.

"Yes, I think after dinner I shall call it a night."

Rupert threw a ball over and over again for the dogs, who ran and fell over each other in the snow. It was a welcome relief from the case.

Dusk began falling and *Knightsbrooke Priory* darkened into a giant, black block in contrast to the shimmering snow. As Rupert called the dogs, a car rolled onto the long avenue and Dodo watched the headlights dip and rise with interest. It pulled to a crunchy stop in front of the portcullis and the chauffeur jumped out to open the back door. An older man emerged whose face was eerily familiar. The hook on the bridge of his nose and the heavy brow left no doubt that Dodo was looking at the son of Lady Marlborough.

Rupert moved forward to shake his hand. "Lord Marlborough. I hope your journey was not too bad."

"No snow till we reached Leicestershire, thankfully." His booming voice made Dodo wonder if he was slightly deaf.

"Dashed inconvenient having to come on Christmas Day."

So sorry we couldn't arrange for the murders to better suit your calendar.

"Quite, quite," murmured Rupert. "If you would like to follow me."

When Lord Marlborough entered the drawing room, he headed straight for his mother.

"William!" she cried, leaning into his neck in a rather dramatic manner. It was like watching a stage play.

"Oh, William," she cried again, lifting her face. "I feel so much better now you are here."

Lord Marlborough unpeeled himself from his mother's embrace and looked around the room with small, hooded eyes. His gaze caught on Mr. Danforth's, and he crossed the room to shake his hand. Lord Marlborough was a good three inches shorter.

Intrigued to know the progress of the fingerprint project, Dodo slipped from the room.

"How does this work in practice," she asked the inspector, whose desk was scattered with several sheets of inky paper.

"Using this magnifying glass, I compare the prints found on surfaces, like the cyanide tin or suicide note, to the prints I have taken, looking for similar patterns. Everyone's fingerprints contain arches, whorls, and loops."

"What a painstaking process." She sighed.

"Yes, it is rather," Inspector Allingham agreed, pinching the bridge of his nose and leaving a smudge of ink. "Still, it's better than nothing."

"Rather you than me, Inspector. You must be exhausted. Have you been to bed since you arrived?"

He put the magnifying glass down on the desk. "No, but another inspector should be here to relieve me within the hour, and I'll get a bit of shut eye."

"I'm glad to hear it. And unless you have any objections, I'm off to bed straight after dinner. I can hardly keep my eyes open."

A quick knock was followed by Lizzie. "I found something. You'd best come right away."

The inspector and Dodo shared a look of exasperation but followed Lizzie to the kitchens and into a large storage room that housed copper pots, silver candlesticks, and bowls. In the center of the room was a large table containing polishing items.

"I had come down to get a few things ready for you before bed," Lizzie began, looking at Dodo, "and I wanted to stay out of the way of the staff since they are understandably a little tense and taking on more responsibilities with the cook out of commission. So, I came to this room they call the butler's pantry." She raised her hands. "Sometimes I'm all fingers and thumbs and I dropped a spoon. When I bent down to pick it up, my eye caught on something. I knelt down to get a better look and saw some crystals that look awfully like the cyanide ones in the tin." She pointed to a corner of the floor by the table leg and Inspector Allingham bent his rotund body down, his joints cracking like old wood on a fire.

The light was bad, and he had to get on his hands and knees and lean in to smell the crystals.

"Yes!" he declared. "Bitter almonds. I need a picture of this. Let's block off the room."

"Lizzie, you've done it again!" cried Dodo. "Since the cook hasn't used the stuff in years, it had to be dropped by the murderer. Well done!"

Lizzie dropped her head.

The inspector unfolded himself with difficulty. "How likely is it that a guest of the family could come into the butler's pantry without being noticed?"

"Very unlikely, I should say," said Dodo. "Whenever I go into the kitchens everyone stops working and curtsies. And they wouldn't know where this room was for a start. No, I think that eliminates the vicar and Lady Marlborough. Don't you agree, Lizzie?"

"I do, m'lady."

Dodo shivered. "Drat! That leaves the family. It's dashed awkward."

The inspector closed the door and dragged a chair in front of it after informing the kitchen staff that it was off limits until further notice.

As they were going back to the main house, there was a heavy knock on the great front door that echoed down the stone passageway. Curious to inspect who it was, Dodo entered the foyer to see a man who could only be Inspector Allingham's replacement.

"Harris!" said the inspector, who had followed her.

The younger man doffed his hat and snowflakes drifted to the floor. "I got here as fast as I could. My wife was none too keen on me leaving on Christmas evening, but the young'uns had opened their presents right early, and they were nigh on asleep as soon as we'd had supper."

"You don't know how glad I am to see you!" announced Allingham. "I've been up for almost thirty-six hours, and I'm hardly able to think straight anymore. Let me fill you in and then I'll get a little shut-eye while you carry on studying the fingerprints."

Dodo cleared her throat.

"Where are my manners?" said Inspector Allingham, gesturing to her with his hand. "This is Lady Dorothea Dorchester. She is one of the guests but more importantly she is an experienced investigator and has been working with me on the case."

Inspector Harris' fine eyebrows lifted but he held out his hand to shake hers. "Good evening, m'lady."

"Good evening, Inspector Harris. I'm so glad the poor inspector, here, will be able to get some sleep. I haven't been up as long as him, but I didn't get a lot of sleep either, and I'm feeling a bit light-headed. I hope you will excuse me going to bed straight after dinner. I will be happy to tell you all I know tomorrow."

"Very good, m'lady." He nodded a full head of burnished hair.

Feeling much refreshed after an uninterrupted night, Dodo awoke with a healthy appetite and figured that scullery maids could not wreck breakfast.

Being the first one down, she ate with abandon, her notebook out on the table.

She began listing all the suspects. She would put Lady Marlborough and the vicar at the bottom since the discovery in the butler's pantry seemed to rule them out. The image of the bulky, unsteady Lady Marlborough light footing it down the stairs, her cane held high, poking around the larder for the cyanide in view of all the staff, put a smile on her face. Likewise, the young, reasonably good-looking vicar would certainly have caught the young maids' attention.

She wrote *Henrietta Danforth*. Was it because of her animosity toward Dodo that she was first on the list? Maybe.

Has lived under the same roof as her mother-in-law for twenty years. Why kill her now? The will did not surprise her. What is the story of her brother's death? Could it be connected? If she was going to kill anyone it would be me with a dagger.

She felt a secret smile on her lips as she wrote the last sentence but crossed it out as it seemed rather catty.

Rupert Danforth II. He was not as openly hostile as his wife, but she wasn't sure she had made great strides with him either. *No apparent bad blood between him and his mother. Was he concerned that she would cut his son out of the will?* From what Rupert had told her, she doubted it was a viable concern.

Ruby Quintrell. As far as Dodo could tell, they had only come for Christmas because Adelaide had told them she altered her will in their favor and they wanted to pay homage. *In desperate need of money. Mother had promised her a healthy allowance or the entire fortune. Interruption of those plans would have been devastating. She would certainly know where the larder and butler's pantry were.* She considered Ruby going into her childhood kitchen. Would her presence raise a brow? Probably. *Might she know how to sneak in without being noticed? Maybe. Means, motive,* and *opportunity.* Dodo tapped her lips with her pencil. *But does a normal person really murder their own mother?*

95

Lawrence Quintrell. Rupert's uncle was forgettable. He had been neither nice nor rude to Dodo—he had been nothing. *Facing financial ruin. Been in the family for over twenty-five years. Undoubtedly knows the layout of the house including the servants' quarters. Ask David Bellamy if he knows any scuttlebutt.*

David was a personal friend who was a fount of gossip regarding the upper classes.

She hesitated. She did not really have the heart to include Rupert and his sisters on the list, but a professional investigator must be impartial.

Beatrice Danforth. She considered how far Beatrice had come in her recovery from opium addiction. But she was not so naïve as to believe that addicts never slipped up. *Troubled with opium. Did grandmother not approve and threaten to cut her out of the will?*

From what Rupert had told her, the girls did not expect anything from their grandmother as it was accepted that the bulk of the wealth would be kept intact and given to Rupert.

Julia Danforth. Dodo smiled as she thought of the lively girl who had accepted her immediately. *If she was going to kill anyone it would be over the Reverend Valentine.*

She doodled a heart before finally writing Rupert's name.

Rupert 'Rupie' Danforth III – heir to Knightsbrooke Priory. Her mind wandered to the delicious kiss under the mistletoe, and she indulged herself for a few minutes.

Heir apparent to grandmother's fortune. Used to grandmother threatening to change her will and didn't lay much store by it but does know the layout of the kitchens.

She dug the point of the pencil into the paper. When it came to means, pretty much everyone made the cut since the poison was not kept under lock and key.

"Hello, gorgeous!"

Dodo guiltily flipped the book closed and lifted her cheek for Rupert to kiss.

"How are you feeling today?" he asked.

"Much better thank you. It never ceases to amaze me how much a proper sleep helps when one is emotionally and physically drained." She tilted her head. "I must confess, I had rather sweet dreams of that kiss. Perhaps we can schedule a repeat performance today?"

Rupert's face split into a heart-stopping grin. "I think that can be arranged, m'lady."

He went to the silver salvers and filled his plate with breakfast delights. As he sat down, he asked her, "Have you spoken to either of the inspectors this morning?"

"No. Neither one. You?"

"Let's go and get an update after we eat."

"Super!" She watched as Rupert filled his perfect mouth with delicious, thick, fragrant bacon. "Tell me about your aunt and uncle."

He took a deep breath. "They never have any money. I know for a fact they have borrowed money from Father. He tells me because one day the estate will be mine. We'll never see a penny of it, of course." His lips twisted and he lowered his voice. "Keep this under your hat, but Uncle Lawrence has an illegitimate son."

Dodo choked on her coffee. "No!" She wiped her mouth with a napkin. "Does your aunt know?"

Now it was Rupert's turn to choke. "Not likely! She'd kill him—oh!" His face fell. "That was insensitive of me under the circumstances."

Dodo was still reeling at the idea of the homely, pot-bellied man having an out of wedlock son. "How do *you* know?"

"The boy is about ten," Rupert replied. "It happened during a low time in their marriage. He swears he doesn't see the mother anymore but when the boy turned eight, she demanded that he be sent to a good school or she would turn up at the house, son in tow. Uncle Lawrence was terrified and came to see father, laying it all on the table. Father agreed to pay for the boy's schooling at a lesser boarding school if he swore never to be unfaithful again."

Dodo chewed her cheek. "How do you feel about mistresses? In general, I mean. They seem to be a national pastime among the British gentry."

Rupert laid down his knife and fork and faced her, taking her hand in his. "I value fidelity above all else. My father has led by example. I would never betray my wife."

She dropped her eyes in the heat of his stare and flicked her head. "I'm very glad to hear it. It would be a definite stumbling block for me. Once a commitment has been made, I demand absolute fidelity…and I give it."

He rubbed his thumb over hers and the tension in the air fizzled out.

"I'm glad we are in agreement," he said with a playful smile.

Dodo pushed her dirty plate away; the idea of a second helping had fled.

"This makes your uncle's motive even stronger," she murmured. "The boy will need to attend college in a few years. If he thought your grandmother had named them as the main beneficiaries and then heard that she might name someone else, that would give him a stronger reason to stop her before she had time to follow through."

"I suppose you're right," Rupert conceded. "But look at the man! Does he look like the kind of person that could poison an old lady?"

"Rupert, Rupert, Rupert," she began. "How many times have I told you that anyone can be a murderer under the right conditions?"

He shook his head but remained quiet.

"We also need to consider that the person who killed your grandmother, killed the maid too. Warren was obviously a threat to the murderer because of what she witnessed."

Julia bounced into the sunny room. "Happy Boxing Day!" she said, practically dancing. "I don't suppose we can, in good conscience, celebrate, can we? I had so many plans."

"No," said Rupert smiling at his youngest sister. "But perhaps we can steal away for a walk and make a snowman where no one will see it."

Her blue eyes snapped up with excitement burning in them. "Really? That would be marvelous. I shall go mad if I have to stay inside all day."

Julia sat at the table with five pieces of toast dripping with jam and butter. "By the way, they've taken both the bodies away. I saw them leaving as I was coming down the stairs."

"Well, that's a small mercy," said Rupert. "I'm not prone to fears of ghosts or anything but having two murdered bodies in the house is enough to spook anyone."

"Two?" asked Julia.

Rupert, realizing his mistake, looked sideways at Dodo who wrinkled her nose. The facts surrounding Warren's demise had not been made public yet. The inspector agreed that acceptance of the suicide narrative would lead the killer into thinking they had got away with both murders and keep the other guests and family safer.

"Slip of the tongue," he said.

"I'm going to see the inspector," said Dodo, putting down her napkin and pushing back her chair.

"I'll join you," said Rupert. "And then, I'll come and find you for that walk," he said, addressing Julia.

"Idiot!" growled Rupert.

"I think she believed you," said Dodo. "It will probably come out sooner or later."

Both inspectors were huddled together in the study, pieces of paper containing chicken scratch strewn across the fabulous antique desk. Dodo cringed on spying tell-tale smudges of ink across its surface. Dodo was sure they had no idea of its value.

"Any good news from the fingerprint escapade?" she asked as she and Rupert sat down across from them.

Inspector Harris sported a healthy five o'clock shadow and unattractive bags under his eyes. He threw a suspicious glare at Rupert.

"Oh, he's alright," Dodo assured him. "Adelaide was always threatening to change her will, so Rupert laid little store by it."

The recent arrival looked unconvinced.

Inspector Allingham patted his colleague on the shoulder. "She's right," he confirmed. His face had been cleared of exhaustion but the same could not be said for his clothes.

"Most of the prints were smudged," Allingham continued, "and those that weren't, were the ones you would expect to see. And as I told you, the food and wine you confiscated did not test positive for cyanide. I would therefore draw the preliminary conclusion that it was given to her a little *before* dinner. Though I do not discredit your knowledge on the matter, Lady Dorothea, I thought it best to consult a doctor for an expert opinion on how long the poison would need to take effect. He agreed with your conclusion—five to fifteen minutes from ingestion. The tricky thing is working out when that was."

"The eggnog!" cried Dodo. "We had it after the church service, before dinner. I had forgotten, but Adelaide brought hers into the dining room. I remember I thought it was amusing that she flaunted the rules that way."

"Granny had a weakness for the stuff," agreed Rupert.

"That would certainly have been strong enough to cover the taste of the poison," Dodo said. "After we came back from the service, everyone except the vicar, who was still at the church, and myself, went to socialize with the old ladies who had chosen to stay behind. Any one of them could have slipped something into Adelaide's cup. However, who knows when she actually took a sip after the poison was administered?"

"What happened to *that* glass?" asked Inspector Harris.

"No idea," said Dodo, twisting her lips with regret. "I didn't see any other glass by her setting after her passing. One of the footmen must have whisked it away during dinner since it was out of place. Then it would have been washed and put away. Drat!"

"Water under the bridge, m'lady," said Inspector Allingham, kindly. "We know what the poison was and where it was stored. Being able to produce the evidence of residue in the glass would be icing on the cake."

"Still," she said. "It is thoroughly exasperating."

"What about the suicide letter?" asked Rupert, changing the subject. "We know that is a fake, correct?"

"Now that is a little different. There were no fingerprints on it at all which is highly suspect. It means the killer wore gloves and took great care not to pollute the page," said Inspector Harris.

"Unfortunately, the paper has no distinguishing features or watermark so that doesn't help us either. But the lack of fingerprints and the fact that it is a forgery both validate that this was a pre-meditated murder. The maid was silenced."

"That is something I suppose." Dodo glanced at Rupert. "And what about Mrs. Danforth's brother? Did you find out anything about his drowning?"

Rupert jumped in. "Uncle Oliver?" he asked, his brow furrowed. "What has that got to do with anything?"

"Sometimes murders are committed because of something that happened in the past," Dodo explained.

Rupert shifted forward in his seat. "You suspect my mother?" An emotional door slammed shut between them and her stomach twisted. "Just because she's acting a little strange does not make her a murderer."

"I told you, murder was messy," she said as gently as she could. "Would you rather not be involved in the investigation, Rupert? We have to suspect everyone. It is the scientific method and at times it will leave a very nasty taste in the mouth."

Rupert considered for a moment his jaw clenching. "I see what you're saying," he finally said. "But I don't like it."

"It is the only way to clear the mist and find the truth," she said, painfully aware that the two officers were watching them with undisguised interest.

Rupert crossed his arms. "Uncle Oliver died before I was born."

Dodo released a breath.

Inspector Allingham picked up a paper. "I asked your mother about it, but she was not particularly forthcoming, so I asked two constables to look at the newspaper archives. They weren't too happy about research on Christmas, I can tell you." He laughed, but no one else did and he cut it off half-way. "The death was ruled an accident," he explained. "Your mother and father and some friends were spending a lazy day at the lake, here in the grounds of *Knightsbrooke Priory*."

Dodo thought of the lake she had barely been able to make out under the snow. *Oliver Forsythe died here?*

"The report says there were only two row boats, so they were all taking turns and picnicking on the banks," continued the inspector. "One boat was out, when those on the bank heard a cry and a splash from the middle of the lake. Their view was obscured by tall bulrushes but only one occupant made it back to the side of the lake alive. Your mother's brother couldn't swim apparently and went under quickly when the boat capsized. It is not clear how that happened. The other occupant of the boat tried to swim down to get Oliver, but his foot was caught in the reeds at the bottom of the lake. After trying for several seconds, he surfaced to fill his lungs with air but when he went down again, your mother's brother had drowned. He managed to untangle Oliver's foot and get him back into the boat, but it was too late."

"How awful!" declared Dodo, a kernel of sympathy growing for Henrietta.

"This story is vaguely familiar," said Rupert. "Mother doesn't talk about the specifics often, but I've heard this before. She and Oliver were very close. I do know she postponed the wedding to father because she was mourning so deeply."

"Who was the other person in the boat?" asked Dodo.

Inspector Allingham looked straight at Rupert.

"Your grandfather."

Chapter 13

"What! I've never heard that!" cried Rupert, dragging his hands through his hair. "It can't be true!"

All eyes in the room were on him, waiting for his acceptance. "Are you sure?"

Inspector Allingham clasped his hands and stared at Rupert over them. "Positive."

"That is perhaps one of the reasons why it is not spoken about," suggested Dodo.

The inspector was still staring at Rupert as if waiting for him to come to a conclusion.

Dodo swung her gaze beside her and saw the color draining from Rupert's face like water from a canal lock. "I say, are you suggesting that my mother killed my grandmother because she suspected that my grandfather had not done enough to save her brother over twenty-five years ago?"

"We are not suggesting anything," said Inspector Harris. "We are laying out the facts as we know them."

Rupert seemed unable to stop shaking his head. "I need some time to wrap my head around this explosive revelation," he said, pushing his chair back roughly and making for the door. Dodo jumped up to follow him.

"Excuse us, gentlemen."

She had to run to catch up with Rupert who was striding to go outside.

"Rupert!" she called.

He did not stop, and a sick feeling uncurled inside her. "You do see that everyone's background must be dug through," she pleaded.

"Bulldozed you mean," he said, glaring at her with those eyes. "I didn't even know it happened here at *Knightsbrooke*. Why wouldn't they tell us?" Unshed tears shone in the morning light, and she wanted to hug him and tell him everything was going to be alright. But she couldn't. She did not know if that was the truth.

He finally stopped on the edge of a courtyard at the back of the castle, staring in the direction of the lake. "Mother never came to the lake. It was always Father who fished and rowed with us."

Dodo had run out without a coat and shivered.

"Would you lay all that on an impressionable child?" she asked quietly.

"When you put it like that…" His brow creased, reflecting the mental anguish he was suffering. "No wonder my mother is touchy about it."

Dodo's teeth chattered and he pulled her to him. "On the plus side, that means her anger toward you is not personal." He kissed the top of her head. "The murders have just harrowed up buried memories that are best left untouched."

She looked sideways at him. "I beg to differ. The way she looks daggers at me is very personal."

"But you have to admit how hard this must be for her. To be reminded." He ran a hand down his anxious face. "Poor Mother."

Poor me, too.

"It does appear only to have been a terrible accident, though," she said. "And her brother didn't swim."

"Ghastly."

Julia appeared in the courtyard, trussed up in warm clothes, ignorant of the moment she was interrupting. "Ready to make a snowman, Rupie?"

Dodo witnessed Rupert try to wipe the anguish from his face so as not to disappoint his sister and fell a little more in love. "Of course." He looked at Dodo. "Do you want to come?"

The snow had stopped but a brisk wind was sending flakes flying across the top of the downy landscape and bending the trees. Besides, she didn't want to monopolize Rupert.

"No. You two go and have fun."

Julia grabbed his hand. "Let me get a coat and gloves," he said, and they hurried back inside.

The two gloomy, black towers stood like sentinels, an omen of bad things to come.

Dodo glanced at the time, her teeth chattering uncontrollably. Eleven. It was as good a time as any to call David.

There was a lot of noise in the background, and someone was playing Christmas tunes on the piano rather badly. "Oh yes, I've heard of old Lawrence Quintrell," shouted David. "He owes quite a lot of money to a close friend of mine. He's terrible at cards."

"Are you having a party, David?"

"Just a few friends for some harmless games on Boxing Day. There may be a few cocktails thrown in for good measure."

"It's eleven o' clock in the morning," she pointed out.

"But it's a holiday. Fair game, I say."

Dodo tutted. "Anything else of interest about him?"

"Who is he to you, if you don't mind me asking?" David was already slurring his words a little.

"He's Rupert's uncle. Married to his father's sister."

"And what has the old chap done?"

"Nothing as far as I can tell."

"What are you not telling me, darling?" She could hear the suspicion in his question.

"Well…"

David slapped something. "Are you embroiled in another murder?"

"You make it sound like people are dropping all around me," she protested.

"Because they *are*, darling! You're worse than the bubonic plague!"

She laughed. "Really David, you're being rather overdramatic."

"From where I'm sitting, I'm the master of understatement. Who died this time?"

"Rupert's grandmother and one of the guest's lady's maids."

"Two murders! Oh well, that is precious! What a jolly Christmas *you* are having." He exploded into guffaws fueled by alcohol.

She waited.

"Are you done?" She dropped her voice. "Is it common knowledge that Mr. Quintrell has an illegitimate son?"

David sobered up quickly. "No! But it is now."

"David," she warned. "This is all in confidence. You cannot tell anyone about this. Do I have your promise?"

"I swear on my mother's grave that I will not tell anyone"—a smacking sound indicated that someone had kissed his cheek very close to the mouthpiece of the telephone—"the information you just imparted."

"Thank you. I'm helping the police to gather information on the people in the house."

His tone turned steely. "How can you be sure it isn't Rufus?"

"Rupert," she corrected. "Because it's not."

"I see how it is," he snorted.

"Back to Lawrence Quintrell. Do you know anything else about him?"

"He's just a bit of an empty shell who always loses at cards. I've never heard of him being violent if that's what you're asking."

"It is. Of all the people it could be, he is the one I really *want* it to be because the alternatives are just too horrible."

"Poor Dodo. Not much of an introduction to the family, is it?"

"You don't know the half of it! Rupert's mother hates me!"

"Surely not. You are so loveable."

She heard a horn being blown. "She seems to think I brought a curse on the house."

"This just gets better and better." he chuckled.

"Shut up, David! I'm serious. Her brother drowned as a young man, and she's funny about death, and when she found out about my sleuthing, an impenetrable wall went up. Then when her mother-in-law was killed, I became a pariah."

"Sounds grim. You should come down here and join my party."

"As lovely as that sounds"—something crashed on the piano in the background making a racket— "I need to stay here with Rupert and try to help the police sort this out as soon as possible. It's the only way I can get back into Mrs. Danforth's good graces."

"Yes, I see that. I hope he's worth it, darling."

"He is. David..." She paused. "I think he might be the one."

She heard another slapping sound and a groan. "Then there's no chance for me? I shall have to drown my sorrows."

"Sounds like you have made a pretty good start on that already. I'll talk to you soon." She kissed the air and hung up.

The picture of Lawrence Quintrell just got worse and worse.

Lord Marlborough started to get to his feet as Dodo entered the room. She quickly indicated that it was unnecessary, whereupon he sank back into the furniture with a grunt.

"Dashed business this," he declared, grabbing his white, whiskered mustache between his fingers and running them to the ends. The dogs eyed him with suspicion.

"Yes. I'm sure your mother didn't expect to lose her friend over Christmas, and in such a violent fashion."

Lord Marlborough was nursing a tumbler of whiskey which he now raised in his chubby hand. "Jolly good stuff this," he declared. "Makes up for the wrath of the wife, don't you know."

He knocked back a gulp and smacked his lips.

"I understand you knew Adelaide Danforth yourself," Dodo began.

"Yes, yes," he huffed. "I did some business for her some years ago and she said she would reward me with a little something after she died." He stared through his long, unwieldy eyebrows. "But Mother told me she did nothing of the kind. Cheeky tactic if you don't mind me saying so."

"Indeed. If it helps, you were not the only one to be bamboozled."

He tipped the crystal glass and emptied it into his wide mouth. "That doesn't surprise me."

"I believe your mother and Adelaide were childhood friends," she said, to prolong the conversation.

"Ever since they were whippersnappers! In each other's pockets by all accounts."

"I heard she even introduced your mother to your father."

"Yes, I'd forgotten." He stroked the mustache, staring into the fire. "Funny to think that."

"Your mother mentioned that they lost touch sometime after your uncle died."

Lord Marlborough frowned. "Uncle Cedric? Yes, yes. Sad that was. I wasn't born but he and Mother were very close—but most twins are."

"They were twins?" Dodo was shocked by this piece of information.

"Oh, yes. Mother was the strong one and mothered Cedric. She was inconsolable when he died, by all accounts."

"I heard it was from heart failure."

Lord Marlborough nodded. "It was weakened by a bout of scarlet fever so that when he became ill a few years later it failed completely. He slipped away after three days hanging between life and death."

The door burst open, and a red-cheeked Julia rushed in followed by Rupert, bringing a burst of cold air with them.

"You'll have to come and see it tomorrow, Dodo. Our snowman is marvelous," gushed Julia. "We gave him a wooly hat and sticks for arms."

"I shall." She gestured with her arm. "I was just chatting with Lord Marlborough."

Julia's smile melted and she nodded to the unobserved guest. "Excuse me, I didn't see you there."

"How is your mother doing?" asked Rupert.

"She was in a frightful state when I arrived, but I arranged for some brandy which soothed her nerves. She even managed to eat a late breakfast and is now taking a much needed nap."

"And how is your room? Do you need anything?"

"No, it is quite comfortable now that the fire has heated the place up." He looked around. "Fine old place this. Fifteenth century?"

"Thirteenth actually," and Rupert launched into the history of *Knightsbrooke Priory*.

Julia and Dodo found a seat in a corner of the room, allowing the men time to converse.

"This is the worst Christmas I can remember," Julia complained. "But it started off so well. And now we have a funeral and that will put a damper on New Year's. Gosh!" She covered her mouth with her palm. "That sounds awfully selfish of me, but I know that Granny wouldn't want to spoil our fun."

"I'm sure she wouldn't," agreed Dodo. "But you must give her a proper send-off."

"Of course." Julia stared out of the small window. The sun was hidden by clouds again and the landscape looked uninviting.

"Where is Beatrice? I haven't seen her today," remarked Dodo.

"I think she's reading in the solar where Mummy is taking a nap," She ran a finger down the window. "Rupert told me how much you helped Bea."

Dodo would wager that Rupert hadn't told her the half of it.

"But she is still not back to normal," Julia continued. "I miss the old Bea. *She* was always the one to plan adventures and she would have been the first to suggest building a snowman."

"Give it time. She's on the mend. She certainly brightens up when the vicar is here." Dodo decided to bring the rivalry out of the shadows to see how Julia was coping after their little heart to heart.

"Yes, she does," growled Julia, her delicate cheeks drooping.

"I don't know what she sees in him," said Dodo. "He really is quite ordinary."

Julia's eyes got wide as if Dodo had just blasphemed. "How can you say that? He is so handsome and intelligent."

"Posh!" declared Dodo. "You just haven't had much exposure to good looking young men. When I was at school there was a maintenance man who was probably thirty. He was reasonably attractive but more so because we were starved of male companionship. He didn't deserve all the attention he got. It makes me laugh when I look back now."

Julia tipped her head. "I've thought a lot about what you said yesterday. Do you think it's just a crush?"

"I would place good money on it. When you come up to London, I'll take you to some parties and you will forget all about the Reverend Valentine."

Julia slid her eyes right while her lips went left. "Let's hope so. I'm so tired of feeling jealous."

Lady Marlborough waddled in and made straight for her son. Dodo squeezed Julia's hand and then sloped over to the sofa with the others.

"I didn't know you were a twin," Dodo remarked as she settled next to Rupert. "My cousins are twins."

Lady Marlborough's eyes snapped up and she forced a smile onto her lined and wrinkled face. "Yes," she replied. "I thought I might have twins myself because of that. Never did."

"Losing a brother or sister must be very hard but losing a twin seems worse, somehow."

The old lady's cloudy eyes narrowed. "It is." She smoothed her voluminous skirts. "Is it too early for tea?"

"We are living in unusual times," replied Rupert. "I'll order some right away."

Chapter 14

Inspector Allingham appeared at the door and indicated to Dodo that he would like a word. He was looking even more rumpled, having now worn the same clothes for some forty-eight hours, but his expression was all business.

Inspector Harris was waiting for them in the study.

"We have confirmed that the crystals your maid found in the servants' quarters were cyanide. We've questioned the staff again, specific to that, and they do not remember anyone unexpected coming into the kitchen that day. But at least we know that it *was* taken from the kitchen supply."

No one unexpected?

The comment set Dodo's mind twirling.

She snapped her fingers. "How about this? Knowing that it would cause a stir if any of the family or the guests went into the kitchens, someone might have asked Lady Marlborough's maid to get the cyanide for them, citing a problem with mice in their room."

The two policemen looked at each other and Inspector Allingham nodded slowly. "Let's take that theory a little further. The killer uses the excuse of vermin and then Adelaide Danforth dies. Two separate events. She's a very old lady and except for the inconvenience of her demise being at Christmas, no one would have been suspicious, and her death would have been put down to natural causes. But Lady Dorothea happened to be here and noticed some things that led her to suspect that Adelaide had been poisoned. After her theory was supported by our investigation, Warren the maid makes the connection and is conscience stricken."

"That is one theory," said Dodo. "I take a rather darker opinion of human nature, Inspector. Remember my maid suggested that Warren may have seen it as an avenue for blackmail?"

Inspector Harris became animated. "Either way, the murderer would fear that Warren would give them away and see the need to silence her."

Inspector Allingham stroked his ample chin. "Could be, could be."

"I have also recently discovered something else that might be relevant," Dodo admitted. "Mr. Quintrell is up to his elbows in debt from gambling at cards and…" She paused for dramatic tension. "I have it on good authority that he has an illegitimate son."

She couldn't have asked for a more perfect reaction from the inspectors. Incredulity morphed into confusion as the ramifications of her revelation distilled.

"How in the world did a funny looking chap like that—?" Inspector Allingham seemed to realize the inappropriate nature of his comments and swallowed the rest of the words.

"Be that as it may, Inspector, he is the father of a ten-year-old son, whose mother has demanded that he be properly educated or else she will reveal the child's existence to Mr. Quintrell's wife. Combine that with bad investments and enormous debt and you have a pretty good motive for murder, I'd say."

Inspector Allingham tipped his head to Inspector Harris. "Let's get Mr. Quintrell in here before you head out."

With her head on Rupert's shoulder and his arm around her she could temporarily forget about all the madness. She had filled him in on her discussion with the policemen. At first Rupert had been worried that she had shared the secret of his uncle's son but when she pointed out that this was the strongest motive to date to prevent his grandmother from changing her will and took the spotlight off his mother, he saw the light.

They were now sitting in the solar, alone. The sky was bright, the sun was shining in, and their fingers were interlaced.

"I'm still dazed from learning that my grandfather was in the boat with my uncle when he died," he murmured.

"It was a bit of a shock," she agreed. "Are you going to mention it?"

"Not on your life! It's obviously something Mother and Father have kept from us and for good reason."

"That's probably wise," she agreed.

"Unless"—he sat up suddenly tense—"and I can barely even go there in my mind—unless you are right, and Mother suddenly couldn't stand it anymore and killed grandmother by association."

"When you put it like that, it's a pretty flimsy motive compared to your uncle's." She ran a finger up his arm. "I'm not saying it's alright that she died but not many people live to be as old as your grandmother. My own is only seventy-two. Adelaide seemed pretty healthy."

"She was and had all her marbles too. I know she had more than her fair share of childhood diseases, chicken pox, scarlet fever, measles— and she lost a baby, but I think it all made her stronger."

"Scarlet fever? Someone else mentioned that. Did you ever have it?"

"There was an outbreak at school when I was eleven, and they sent everyone home to quarantine. Did you?"

"No, but I had a bad case of mumps and measles." They sat in companionable silence for a few minutes then Dodo asked, "What do you usually do on Boxing Day?"

"In the old days father would join a hunt—that was before the war. Now, we sometimes go to the races, but we didn't plan for that this year because we were having guests."

"I am more surprised than ever that we have never met before," she said. "Did you know that my father owns several racehorses?"

"I didn't. Would I know them?" he asked.

"*Arabian Knight* is the most famous."

"What! Everyone knows *Arabian Knight*! I had no idea it was your horse. Isn't it funny that we can live our lives, and pass each other in the street, so to speak, and yet never meet? I have seen him run at least twice."

Dodo put her head on his shoulder. "I don't go every time he runs. Were you there the year *he* was poisoned?"

113

"No, but I remember the story, of course. It was all over the papers," replied Rupert.

"It was my first proper case," she said with a small smile as she remembered the day and how she eventually deduced who the horse poisoner was.

"Really? How clever. How old were you?"

"Barely eighteen. Father asked me to look into it to keep things private."

"I don't think it worked. The papers had a field day, as I recall. I don't remember who the culprit was, though."

"The head groom. It was a terrible day when I realized. He had been with Daddy in the army. He felt the betrayal badly." She stared at the beautiful landscape painting that hung over the mantle, realizing for the first time that it was the view from the roof of *Knightsbrooke*.

"How's the horse?"

"He recovered but there is a small window for being a champion in the Triple Crown and he missed it. He's still good but that year he was at his peak."

"So, you *do* like horses," declared Rupert.

"I didn't say I didn't like horses, I said I didn't like *riding*," she protested.

"I shall have to do something about that this summer." He tickled her hand and wrapped his foot around hers.

"If you are a good boy, perhaps Daddy will let you ride *Arabian Knight*."

"Do you really think he'd let me? That would be wonderful."

They turned their heads in tandem as the door opened and Dodo immediately stiffened.

"Oh!" said Etta in a voice loaded with disappointment. She turned to leave.

"Mother," said Rupert leaping up to usher his mother in. "Don't let us dissuade you. Come in."

She eyed Dodo as if she were an over ripe fish one has found in the back of the refrigerator.

Dodo summoned up her courage. "Do come in," she said with as much bonhomie as she could muster.

Etta paused, eyes sliding between them in indecision.

114

At that very moment the sun increased its power, filling the comfortable room with light and warmth. It was as though the universe was inviting Etta to stay and it proved to be the final push she needed.

"If you insist." She entered holding a book.

"How are you, Mother?" Rupert asked her.

With an expression that reminded Dodo of someone suffering from kidney stones, she shook her head. "Who would do such a thing to your grandmother?" She gripped her neck as if she could find the answers there. "And the poor visiting maid. I just don't understand it all." She had aged ten years since Dodo first met her.

Is it remorse?

"I'm terrified knowing there is a killer in the house and worried for the girls' safety. One should not have to feel this way in one's own home."

"Have the police kept you up to date on their progress?" asked Dodo.

"I am avoiding them as much as possible," she confessed. "It is so intrusive for one thing."

"Perhaps knowing more will ease your mind somewhat," Dodo suggested.

'Scowl' was too nice a word to describe the look that filled Etta's ordinary face.

"I think that's a splendid idea," agreed Rupert. "We can fill you in."

The suggestion from him seemed a lot more palatable and Mrs. Danforth took a deep breath. "Alright." She finally sat in one of the dainty, floral armchairs.

"The poison was taken from an old tin of rat poison in the cold storage pantry. The tin had been pushed to the very back and not used for years," Rupert explained. "This would suggest that the first…incident was a crime of opportunity and not pre-meditated, which makes me feel better somehow."

"Something must have happened on Christmas Eve that was a catalyst," said Dodo. Etta's head stayed firmly turned to her son, but she swung cold eyes over to Dodo. The effect was not welcoming.

Rupert jumped back in. "The police now believe that someone slipped the cyanide into Granny's eggnog which she took into dinner—you know how she loved it."

"It definitely was not given to her in the food or wine at dinner," said Dodo. "The police had them both checked." She omitted her role in that part.

Etta pursed her lips. "Honestly, I don't know how any of this is supposed to make me feel better."

"Knowledge sometimes gives one a feeling of more control," said Dodo.

"Well, it hasn't worked. I feel absolutely helpless." She hugged herself. "Adelaide was a harmless old lady, and what had the maid ever done to anyone? I'm frightened to eat or drink anything. I fear I could be next."

She knows the maid did not commit suicide? That would explain the increase in her fretfulness.

"I think that is unlikely," said Dodo and received a glare for her efforts.

"How do you know?"

"I don't, it's just that the death of the maid suggests that she knew something or had been involved in some way and was killed to keep her quiet. Unless you saw something you shouldn't, you are not a threat to the mur—killer."

Etta ran fingers through her disheveled, graying hair. "I didn't. I know nothing." She groaned. "I just want to escape, leave for a few days, but the inspector has forbidden it. I remember feeling this way about the house once before."

Dodo and Rupert shared a glance. Dodo bounced her foot leaving the silence open for Etta to fill it.

Etta looked at Rupert. "It was when your uncle died."

"Oh?"

"Did you know he died here in the lake?"

"No." A white lie to elicit more information.

"It was before I was married to your father. We had just got engaged and I was visiting the house. Oliver went out on a little punt boat. I told him not to, since he didn't swim, but he never listened to me. He went out to the middle of the lake but from where I was sitting, the bullrushes obstructed the view and I couldn't see him. A good fifteen minutes passed and then we heard a cry and a splash. I jumped up but he was out of view. By the time anyone got to him…" She stared out of the large window into the bright sun. "…it was too late."

Rupert's brow knitted. "Was he alone?"

His mother turned her head slowly, considering. "You look a lot like him," she murmured. "He and I were very close, and you have given me much solace when I have missed him so much it hurts." Her fist went to her chest. "He was my confidante. I used to tell him everything. Then he was gone. I pushed back the wedding to give myself time to grieve. Your father was very patient."

The ticking of the clock became loud as silence descended again and Etta's eyes drooped.

"Why don't you rest, Mother. Come over here and kick up your feet. I can cover you with a blanket."

"That would be nice." He led her to the sofa, and she tipped over slowly, resting her head on the arm of the plush settee, half asleep already, the book slipping from her hand.

Rupert placed a tartan blanket tenderly over her and they started to creep out of the room.

"Yes," his mother murmured.

They stopped, eyes locking.

"Yes?" he asked, seeking clarification.

"Oliver was alone in the boat."

Chapter 15

The significance of what Rupert's mother had just said was not lost on either of them. Was she still shielding Rupert from an uncomfortable revelation or was she really ignorant? It couldn't be the latter—because now they knew she was there! Had she indeed held a grudge all these years and decided to reap her revenge now? By this false statement was she covering her tracks?

A slight twitch had appeared by Rupert's right eye.

He closed the door to the solar but kept his palm on the handle.

"Should I confront her? Tell her that I know that was a lie?" His voice was hoarse with unease and doubt.

"She's tired. Let your mother take a nap and give yourself time to think. Don't do anything rash," advised Dodo, though she couldn't help feeling this denial was a vital clue to this sticky puzzle. Two women in the house had lost a brother in their youth. Could it be a simple coincidence? The ugly fact felt like a nasty itch and Dodo experienced an intense craving to scratch it.

Two deaths in the past, two deaths in the present.

They walked along in silence, each lost in their own thorny thoughts.

When they reached the grand entry hall, the vicar was shrugging out of his coat and hat. He looked up and smiled. In terms of attractiveness, he was a solid average, but Dodo did have to concede that he had a redeeming smile.

"Vicar," said Rupert, pasting a forced smile onto his troubled face. "How fortunate that you have arrived. I'm concerned about my mother. She is taking a short nap but afterwards I think a bit of shepherding might not go amiss."

Was Rupert arranging for a private confessional? Had he moved so far from his preconceived notions of his mother's innocence that he now believed her guilty of the two murders? Even Dodo had not made that leap yet.

118

When Reverend Valentine saw the strain in Rupert's face, he wiped the smile from his own. "Of course. Whatever I can do to help."

Rupert stood back, indicating with his arm for the vicar to walk ahead of him. "Please join us in the drawing room. I apologize, but I don't think there will be a formal dinner this evening, what with everything."

The vicar made a dismissive gesture with his hand. "Think nothing of it. I have merely come to offer solace."

To Beatrice.

Only Rupert's father was in the drawing room, a stern expression stamped on his features which cracked when they entered.

"Vicar," he said. "I think Etta could do with some counsel. I'm worried about her."

Him too!

"I have just this minute suggested the same thing," said Rupert, "but she is catching forty winks in the solar."

"I'm relieved. She has not been sleeping. All this business has stirred up her grief for her brother. She feels tremendously guilty that she invited Oliver here that day and that she wasn't more insistent that he not go on the lake. Have you heard the story?"

The vicar put a finger to his lips. "This is all quite strange, but I *do* know this story."

Dodo's ears perked up. It had not been mentioned in public and unless Beatrice had spoken of it, how could the vicar know?

"You do?" Mr. Danforth's brows curled.

The vicar appeared to hesitate. *What is he hiding?*

"You must understand, I had no idea when I came to Knightsbrooke." He fingered the white collar at his neck. "A few words were dropped after the sad situation with your mother, and certain of them stirred a memory. I called my own mother last night to confirm the recollections those words triggered."

The vicar was making no sense and a strange spirit entered the room.

Rupert conducted the vicar to an armchair. "Please explain yourself."

The vicar sat with his elbows on his knees. "It is a fantastic eventuality when I think about it… but I shall start from the beginning.

"My grandmother was from near here, just over the county line. Her name was Alexandra Matthews. She married Dante Valentine and they had four children. One of whom was my father, Herbert. He married Clarice Byford, my mother."

Rupert's father tilted his head. "Alexandra? Any relation to Humphrey Matthews?"

Was it guilt that suddenly suffused the vicar's face?

"Actually, he's my cousin."

"So, you have family in the area," concluded Rupert's father.

"Yes. It's one of the reasons I jumped at the chance to come here to Knightsbrooke. I have family scattered all over these parts.

"My mother married Herbert Valentine but…" He paused and people in the pictures on the walls seemed to lean in with anticipation. "Before she met my father, she was courting a man called Oliver Forsythe."

A gasp escaped Rupert's father. "You mean my wife's brother?"

"I do."

Rupert gasped.

"When I came home from divinity school one year," the vicar continued, "Mother had a box of old photographs out, photographs I had never seen, and she was crying. It was the first time I had ever heard the name Oliver Forsythe. She was not here at *Knightsbrooke Priory* that fateful day as she had an engagement she could not get out of. But she loved him, and she took the news of his death very hard."

"That is incredible!" spluttered Rupert's father. "And you didn't put the pieces together until after my mother died? I wonder if Etta remembers her?"

"It wasn't until Beatrice mentioned something about the deaths in your family that I made the connection."

"Why didn't you say anything before—about this association with our family?" demanded Mr. Danforth.

120

"Because I have only just had it confirmed," said the vicar in defense. "Don't you see? If my mother had married Oliver, I would have been cousin to your children."

That is startling information, indeed!

Dodo's brain started to churn. Did this give the vicar motive to kill Adelaide Danforth? Was there more that the vicar was withholding? She yearned to find a piece of paper and get her muddled thoughts down.

Rupert's father made a strange gurgling laugh. "It's almost too fantastic. Hard to believe."

"I know!" exclaimed the vicar. "I would have been Dante Forsythe instead of Dante Valentine."

Rupert's father huffed and shook his head. "What a small world."

Beatrice pushed into the room, her face showing that the prickly atmosphere was not just in Dodo's imagination.

"Did I miss anything?" she asked looking from face to face. Someone had actually styled her hair and more than a hint of her former beauty was emerging.

Reverend Valentine, who had stood along with the other men when she entered, raised his arm to waist level. "Actually, yes," he said and repeated his story.

A kaleidoscope of surprise drifted across Beatrice's delicate face.

"Maiden names hide a lot of family history," she said when he was done.

"They do indeed."

As everyone chatted, Dodo allowed her mind to process this new information. She was not totally convinced that the vicar had told the entire truth. What if his mother had known that Adelaide's husband had been in the punt and unable or unwilling to save him? Her experience told her that people rarely gave 'the whole truth and nothing but the truth'.

She re-imagined the scene of Reverend Valentine's mother crying over the picture and telling him that Rupert Danforth I, Rupert's grandfather, had been in the boat at the time. Perhaps her marriage to the vicar's father had been unhappy. If the vicar was very close to his mother, he may have developed a plan right

121

then to avenge his mother, and put his name forth for a living in the area of Knightsbrooke. No one would suspect a vicar as an avenging angel, bent on vigilantism.

She grimaced. Rupert was right—she saw murderers everywhere. Vicars as avenging angels? *Really.*

But this was the kind of information the police would find relevant. She slipped out of the room and down to the study, but it was empty.

She asked a parlor maid if she had seen the inspectors and was directed to the kitchen.

As usual, whenever the upper-class residents of a great house entered the servant's quarters it was like a lioness appearing in a crowd of baby elks. If the servants were sitting, they stood with a speed that was enviable and if not, they stopped, rigid in their tracks, staring at the interloper.

"Don't mind me," she assured them. "I'm just looking for the inspectors."

A wide-eyed scullery maid pointed to the housekeeper's room.

She knocked and entering was surprised to see another of the parlor maids, tears streaming down her face as she faced Inspector Allingham.

"Ah, Lady Dorothea," he said. She noticed that the other inspector was not there.

"I'm sorry, am I interrupting?" she asked.

Allingham looked much like a young man who has been asked to hold a baby for the first time. "Actually, your coming is nothing short of serendipitous. Elsie here has been withholding"—the maid whimpered—"uh, sharing some information with me at the urging of the housekeeper."

Dodo assessed the situation quickly and drew up a chair beside the young girl whose cheeks were shiny with tears. She placed a hand along the back of the maid's chair.

"The inspector won't bite, Elsie. Anything you can tell us may be of the greatest importance."

"Start at the beginning," said the inspector, gently.

"Like I said, I was going to the cold storage on Christmas Eve to get some lard for the cook when I saw the old lady's maid, Warren, slipping through the door holding something. Lady's maids don't go to the cold storage, as a rule, so I stopped and watched from a distance. Her eyes kept flitting about the room, and I stepped behind a wall so she didn't see me."

The inspector held up the tin of magnesium cyanide. "Was this what the maid was holding?"

"Yes." Her eyes dropped to the floor.

"Why on earth—?"

Elsie sobbed, restraining the inspector who checked his tone. "Why didn't you come forward before?"

"I couldn't be sure," she moaned. "I didn't want to get into trouble and then she killed herself so I didn't think it would be helpful."

"Why are you coming now?" asked Dodo in a tone that was smooth as silk.

"Oh, m'lady! The guilt has been eating away at me, and I couldn't do my work properly. The cook thought I was being lazy and yelled at me something terrible, but when I burst into tears, she asked what was bothering me."

"Well, you've done the right thing," said Dodo.

The maid wiped her cheeks with the back of her hands. "It's such a relief to get it off my chest."

"Thank you, Elsie," said Inspector Allingham. "Unless you have anything else to say, you are free to go."

The girl shot out of the room like an archer's arrow.

"This merely confirms that Warren took the cyanide," said the inspector.

"But isn't it nice to have something corroborated in a way that would stand up in court?" Dodo pointed out.

"I suppose so." He went to put his notebook away.

"Don't be too hasty, Inspector. I have also come to tell you something that may be of interest to the case."

Dodo related the vicar's tale.

The inspector slapped his forehead. "Well, I never! That *is* a coincidence, and I don't like those in police investigations."

"Me neither," agreed Dodo. "I hate to suggest that a vicar is lying but I can't help feeling that he revised the truth, somewhat. I'm not saying he was up to anything nefarious, but after learning what he did, he might be excused for being a little curious. For peeking behind the curtain to see what might have been."

The inspector leaned back in the chair, his hands behind his head, and sighed. "This case is a puzzler."

"If only we knew who asked Warren to get them the cyanide," mused Dodo. "Of course, Lady Marlborough is the most obvious candidate but what would be her motive? She can't seriously have believed that Adelaide would give money to her son rather than her own flesh and blood."

"I am of the same mind," declared the inspector. "She doesn't really have a motive. But it could be anyone else and now I feel that we have to add the vicar back to the list."

"Have you discovered anything about Warren's previous employers?" she asked.

Inspector Allingham flicked the pages of his notebook. "Before Lady Marlborough, she worked for the Countess of Braintree who died age ninety-eight, in her sleep. Before that, a Mrs. Richardson who passed away on the Continent—and before you go raising those pretty brows, Warren did not travel with her on that occasion. Prior to that she was just a maid."

"Do any of those families have a connection to the Danforths?"

"The ladies she attended were older than Adelaide Danforth but honestly, I don't have the manpower to dig any farther." He closed the book. "But with this new bit of intelligence you have just given me, it would not surprise me to learn that Warren was actually the illegitimate niece of Oliver Forsythe."

Dodo chuckled. "I know! A houseful of seemingly random people comes together for Christmas, only to be linked together by their histories."

Dodo dragged her hand through the air in front of her eyes like a dramatic actress on the silver screen. "Murdered lady's maid found to be illicit daughter of long deceased Oliver Forsythe."

The inspector let out a bark. "Crikey! Let's hope not!"

Chapter 16

A couple of constables had finally arrived to help with the minutiae of the case and security, and Inspector Allingham decided to re-interview the guests and family now that he had more time, and information in his arsenal. He invited Dodo along as a buffer.

Lady Marlborough sat in the study with them. She was not what one would call a handsome old lady by any standard. Some women's harder edges softened as their hair turned white and their bodies gently swelled, but not so with her. There remained a sharp edge to her that would make any small child a little fearful.

Both gnarled hands were placed atop her handsome walking cane with the crystal head, and her eyes were narrowed at the inspector.

"Warren?" she replied to the inspector's inquiry, exhaling heavily. "She had been with me for seven years. I hate to speak ill of the dead, but it is terribly hard to get good help these days. There are so many alternatives to service since the war." She pursed her lips. "Let me think. She had been a lady's maid for five years before she came to me. One of her former employers, the Countess of Braintree, died." Her stern eyes snapped up. "I know what you're thinking, Inspector, and you are barking up the wrong tree. The countess was older than me and needed a nurse more than a maid. That was one of the reasons I hired Warren— her experience tending to the elderly. After that she worked for another elderly gentlewoman and…before that she was a maid."

"You're giving the impression that Warren wasn't very good at her job, is that a fair assessment, m'lady?"

The puckered lips and eye lift gave her away. "She was *almost* satisfactory."

Dodo put her hand up to hide a smile.

"And what of her family?"

One dark eye scrunched shut. "She had a brother who died in the war and both her parents were gone. Is that what you mean?"

"She wasn't adopted or anything?"

"Inspector, what a peculiar question!" She fanned herself with a handkerchief drenched in violet toilet water. Dodo wrinkled her nose. "How would *I* know?"

The inspector gave a patient smile. "It's just a line of inquiry that came up. Lady's maids and their mistresses are often close and share personal details."

Lady Marlborough put her hand to her chest. "Not in my case, I can assure you. Best to keep the line between the classes sharp and true, I say."

Dodo thought of her close relationship with Lizzie and suddenly felt sorry for the haughty Warren.

"Did she act strangely at all before she died?"

"I have gone over and over it all in my mind," Lady Marlborough said waving the hankie. "Racking my brain for every nuance and I did remember a curious conversation we had the morning before I found her body in my room."

The inspector leaned forward.

"She said that it made her sad to see others having a family Christmas because all her family had passed on. I told her to stop being maudlin and she said that no one would miss her if she were gone. That's why I was so sure it was suicide. But you seem to think it was not. Why is that if I may be so bold?"

The inspector narrowed his eyes. "The note is a fake."

Dodo watched the old lady's rheumy eyes which widened briefly.

"A fake? But how do you know?" Her voice had risen an octave.

Dodo wondered how much the inspector would disclose.

"I will just say that there is more than one clue that confirms this to be the case."

Lady Marlborough's left brow shot up. "Her death was *staged*? Was it not she who killed poor Adelaide?"

The inspector adjusted his tie. "We do believe that she assisted the murderer in retrieving the poison, but we cannot definitely conclude that she had a hand in the actual killing of Adelaide Danforth."

126

"Then why was she killed, young man?" The inspector was well over fifty, but Dodo supposed that everyone seemed young to people in their nineties.

"To silence her."

Lady Marlborough gripped her throat. "So, the long and the short of it is that you really know nothing and there is still a murderer on the loose? I demand to leave immediately. I could be next."

"Have you received a threat?" he asked.

She hit her cane on the floor. "No, but you make it sound like a mad person is killing off old ladies. My heart is weak, and all this is bringing on palpitations."

"I'm afraid I cannot let anyone leave just yet," said the inspector. "But in terms of your security, *I* am in the house along with other members of the police force, and your son is here."

Lady Marlborough dipped her pendulous chin and regarded the inspector through terrifying brows. "I suppose it would be bad form to point out that Warren was killed under your nose, Inspector."

Dodo glanced at Inspector Allingham to see how he would take this slight.

He coughed and a dash of color appeared on each cheek. "That is so, your ladyship. Perhaps your son can sleep in the room with you?"

Lady Marlborough huffed. "You give me no choice, Inspector. If I die, my blood will be on your hands. Grown men like, my son, are much less prone to obeying their mothers than youngsters, but I shall insist."

Dodo decided to take the conversation in a less menacing direction to save the poor inspector from more humiliation.

"Lady Marlborough, you mentioned that your brother died while young. Can you tell us more about it?"

Lady Marlborough's whole face creased like a prune. "What on earth does that have to do with anything?"

It was time for a dose of diplomacy. "When investigating a crime, we look for patterns. The fact that both you and Mrs. Danforth lost brothers is a pattern that bears examination." She tipped her head with a tight smile.

Lady Marlborough hemmed, raising her hands so that her bracelets tinkled as if with indignation. "I can assure you there is no connection. Etta's brother drowned, right here in the lake, I understand. I was on a grand tour of Italy with my daughter at the time. I remember because I received news of it well after the fact due to the distance, but I felt a kindred empathy for poor Etta as I knew the same pain myself. I sent my condolences." She folded her handkerchief into a neat square. "My own brother died a generation before Oliver Forsythe, the long-term results of a common childhood ailment. No one was to blame. How many people have gone to meet their Maker from the same thing?"

"Scarlet fever, wasn't it?" asked Dodo.

The old lady's voice lost its force. "He actually died of a heart attack, but the scarlet fever left him with a weak heart, yes."

"Who was his wife at the time of his death?" Dodo persisted.

It took Lady Marlborough a minute to bring herself back from the corridors of time. "What? Oh, Matilda Fenchurch. They were childhood sweethearts. She mourned him for two years before remarrying."

"Did they have any children before his death?"

"Funny you should ask that," Lady Marlborough replied. "After his death she became very ill. We all thought it was the shock of losing her young husband but when the symptoms did not let up the doctor was called. He confirmed that Tilly was with child. He was her saving grace."

"What was his name?"

"Algernon Longthorpe. Cedric's son." She wiped the corner of her eye. "He was the spitting image of his father. It would make my heart catch at times. Blond curls, bird's egg blue eyes. He was a solace to us all." Her cheek glistened. "He was full of adventure and traveled back and forth to the Americas." She locked watery eyes with Dodo. "Perhaps you have heard of the SS Atlantic that sank in 1873?"

Dodo shook her head.

"It regularly made the crossing from Liverpool to New York but on that fateful journey the chief officer thought they were going to run out of coal and diverted the ship to Halifax, Nova Scotia where it ran aground on rocks and sank. Poor Algernon is buried there, one of the five hundred and fifty people who lost their lives."

"I am terribly sorry to hear it," said Dodo, sincerely. "Your family has known much tragedy."

Lady Marlborough wiped her nose.

A knock on the door broke the tension. "Mother? Someone told me you were in here. I was wondering when we are—?" Her son stopped, finally registering the somber atmosphere and his mother's tears. "I say, I'm awfully sorry to interrupt." He ran a hand over his shiny head.

"We were just talking about dear Algernon," explained Lady Marlborough.

"Old Algie. Dashed unlucky that. Never wanted to see America myself." He twirled his large mustache and turned to the inspector. "Still, I was wondering when we might be able to leave? My wife is rather anxious…"

"We have a few more things to follow up on. I'll let you know as soon as possible."

Lord Marlborough's smile dropped quicker than a millstone in a pond. "Oh, because I was hoping to take Mother back to my house to salvage what is left of Christmas."

"I understand that it is a difficult time of year, but I have new questions for everyone which gets complicated when people leave. I can assure you we are working as fast as we can."

Lord Marlborough pushed his mustache up to his nose with distaste.

"Right then," said the inspector, standing. "I am done questioning your mother for the present."

Lady Marlborough placed her cane firmly on the floor and struggled to push her voluminous body up from the chair while her son provided leverage. The two look-alikes ambled haltingly out of the study, leaving Dodo and the inspector alone.

Allingham sighed. "I can't keep everyone here indefinitely but the more information I gather the less clear everything seems. If we don't make significant progress soon, I'll have to let everyone go."

129

Peering nervously at each other and sniffing their food, the household ate a simple meal of cold meats for dinner as Dodo had predicted. There was little conversation and almost everyone went back to their rooms as soon as they had eaten. Ruby had aged in the days since her mother had died, and her husband's joyless eyes were haunted by his secrets. *Or his guilt.* He was still suspect number one in Dodo's mind.

The vicar had been allowed to leave to visit a parish family who had just had their ninth baby and Julia and Beatrice were snuggled together under cozy blankets in the drawing room.

"I am so glad he's gone," said Julia glancing sidelong at her sister.

"Who? The vicar?" asked Rupert.

"Yes, he's monopolizing all of Bea's time." Julia pouted. "And he could be a double murderer."

Beatrice put an arm around her sister. "What nonsense," she said with good humor. "Dante would never hurt a fly." Her color was back, and a ready smile danced across her lips. Dodo could hardly believe it was the same girl she had met in London.

"But I'm sorry about spending too much time with him," Beatrice continued. "I really enjoy his company, but I'd much rather do things with you, little sister, now that my energy is returning."

Lizzie entered bearing mugs of hot cocoa.

"Stay," said Rupert.

Lizzie darted a worried look toward Dodo.

Rupert shook his head with a smile. "I know how close you and Dodo are, and I don't see any of the other guests coming back down tonight."

"If you're sure." The frown that wrinkled her brow made Lizzie look anything but sure.

"Oh yes, you must!" declared Beatrice. "I consider you a dear friend after all your help in London. Sit!"

"If anyone else comes I must be allowed to leave," Lizzie insisted, perching on the very edge of the sumptuous furniture.

"Relax," encouraged Dodo. "I shall take full responsibility if we are found out."

Lizzie handed round the big mugs of hot, sweet cocoa. When Beatrice held hers up to her lips, Dodo saw her eyes mist over.

"I was having cocoa with Granny just a few nights ago," she said. "I can hardly believe she's gone. She was such a constant presence in my life."

"Yes, she was," agreed Julia. "She let me do all sorts of naughty things Mummy would never have allowed."

"Such as?" asked Rupert.

"She let me try snuff once when I was curious. Burned my nose and made me choke," she said, laughing at the memory. "If her aim was to put me off the stuff she succeeded."

"Mother would most definitely not have approved," agreed Rupert.

"She let *me* taste champagne when I was eight years old," said Beatrice. "I liked the sweet bubbles so much I drank the rest of hers when she wasn't looking and got tipsy. She quickly put me to bed before Mother found out."

"My grandmother is a bit like that," said Dodo. "She's the one who encouraged me to take the offer to be a fashion ambassador for the House of Dubois. My parents were scandalized but she said that she could see into the future a time when the aristocracy would need to work for a living."

"Grandparents are a bit removed from the responsibility of child rearing and are able to take more risks I suppose," mused Rupert.

"When I was drinking cocoa with her before she died, she was telling me about a time she disobeyed her own mother," said Beatrice.

"Oh, do tell," begged Julia. "It is so nice to talk about Granny like this, and I'm tired of having to be on my guard all the time. With all of you I can be at ease for a while."

Beatrice wrapped her fingers around the warm mug. "Granny was just nineteen and her parents were hosting a Christmas ball. She had looked forward to it for months and was eager to dance

131

with a certain young man. It was 1849 and she was allowed a new dress for the occasion after the style of one the queen had worn.

"The day of the ball she woke up feeling achy and by the afternoon her cheeks were flushed and her mother told her that she could not in good conscience let her attend. Granny threw a mighty tantrum but her mother would not be moved and she was banished to her room."

"I cannot see that keeping Granny down," said Julia.

"It didn't! She bribed her maid with candied fruit to come and dress her and bring some face powder from her mother's room to cover up the redness of her cheeks. When she was sure the dancing had begun and the room would be filled with people, she sneaked down the stairs and found Millicent—Lady Marlborough now—as if nothing was wrong. When they asked where she had been, she lied and said she had been set a commission by her mother that made her late.

"Lady Marlborough's brother was encouraged to dance with her as he had already danced a set with his new wife. Granny readily agreed hoping that she might catch a glimpse of the young man she wanted to dance with."

"And did she?"

"Yes. The young fellow danced with her five times that night which was completely against the rules, and she managed to stay out of her mother's way until the end of the evening when she ran up the stairs claiming to be tired so as not to be caught as the crowds thinned."

"I can see it now," said Rupert, nodding.

"I bet my grandmother would have done the same thing," declared Dodo. "Did Adelaide recover soon after?"

"No. She was ill for the next week and her mother finally took her to the seaside to recover."

"What illness was it?" asked Dodo, a strange prescience tingling her neck.

"I'm not sure, measles or mumps or something."

A dew of reasoning was distilling upon Dodo's mind. "Try to think Beatrice."

"Does it really matter?"

132

"It might matter very much," declared Dodo. "It might just be the key to this whole sordid affair."

"Have you had a breakthrough?" asked Rupert.

"One is certainly developing, but I don't want to vocalize it until I have some proof." She jumped up. "I'll be right back."

Scampering up the stairs in a most unladylike fashion, Dodo sank to her knees by the desk in her room, crossing her fingers that with all the drama, the maids had not yet emptied the wastepaper basket. She tipped the bin and several pieces of paper rolled forward. She grabbed each one and spread them out until she found the one, she hoped was there.

"Yes!" she cried and snatched a pencil from the drawer in the writing desk. With the crumpled paper as flat as she could make it, she rubbed the graphite lead over the small sheet. A pattern began to materialize, and her heart caught. She rummaged in her bag for her magnifying glass and studied the message that had emerged.

"Eureka!"

Chapter 18

Casting all propriety to the wind Dodo sped down the stairs and back into the drawing room. She was delighted to see that Lizzie had remained after her abrupt departure, and that the siblings were involving her in their conversation.

"Success?" asked Rupert.

Dodo hugged the paper to her chest. "Yes!"

Rupert patted the seat beside him.

Dodo explained her hypothesis and showed them the incriminating item that would now prove who the murderer was without a doubt. Rupert clapped his hands and the two sisters squealed.

"I would never have guessed," remarked Julia, her eyes wide with surprise. "How clever of you."

Rupert looked at her as a new father might look at his firstborn.

"You are brilliant!" he declared. "And you must go and tell the inspector, this minute."

"Come with me," she said.

She and Rupert went in search of Inspector Allingham and after rehearsing her theory to him and presenting the evidence that would seal the murderer's fate, he threw up his hands in relief.

"Your reputation is well deserved, m'lady. I was beginning to think that the killer was going to get away with it for lack of clues." He glanced at his watch. "Nine o' clock—not too late. I shall call a meeting immediately."

As the clock struck the hour, everyone except the vicar, was gathered in the drawing room as the inspector entered. Lady Marlborough was in her nightgown, hands firmly on the crystal top of her cane, wearing a deep frown and muttering under her breath, but no one else had gone to bed.

Dodo had requested that the inspector take center stage for the denouement. He almost refused believing that since the credit was mostly hers, she should get the recognition. But she insisted.

The fire had been stoked, the curtains pulled and most of the characters in the drama now sat in anxious anticipation, with the exception of Lord Marlborough who sat in easy repose, an aloof spectator of the unveiling of a murderer.

Ruby's face was drawn and harrowed, her husband's pinched and gray.

His anguish will surge threefold when his wife knows all his dirty secrets.

Mrs. Danforth seemed to have succeeded in digging herself partway out of her personal pit of despair, but her eyes still watched Dodo like a hawk.

Will I ever win her over?

Mr. Danforth was studying the faces in the room with a detached interest.

Lord Marlborough sat by his mother and had unwound to the point that his eyes were closed, and a fluttered breathing betrayed that he had dozed off.

"Sorry I'm late," gushed the vicar as he hurried in, nose red, completing the cast of actors in the play.

"What, what?" muttered Lord Marlborough at the disturbance, his beady eyes struggling to open.

Reverend Valentine glanced at Beatrice but seeing no room next to her, shuffled over to stand behind the sofa.

Inspector Allingham entered quietly.

Had he been watching for the final suspect to arrive?

He was immediately the center of everyone's attention as he stood poised, hands behind his back, in front of the enormous hearth. The only indication of his excitement was the slight movement of his fleshy cheeks.

"Thank you for coming," he began in a deep bass. "As you are all aware, this has been a memorable Christmas for all the wrong reasons."

"Hear, hear!" mumbled a few voices.

"What should have been a delightful family Christmas has been marred by not one murder, but two."

135

"Two?" declared Ruby, brows knit looking from face to face. "I thought the maid killed herself."

There had been no official announcement about Warren's death, but the secret had slithered its way to most of the family and guests. Since Ruby and Lawrence had kept to themselves, they had obviously not heard.

"Yes, two," reiterated the inspector, stroking his short mustache. "The murderer staged the maid's death to look like a suicide, but they made a few mistakes." He swung his eyes around the figures in the room. "I will lay out the investigation from beginning to end and all will be revealed."

It was apparent to Dodo that the inspector was rather enjoying his role as Sherlock Holmes.

"When Adelaide Danforth died, late on Christmas Eve, everyone assumed that her time had come. Everyone that is, save for Lady Dorothea."

Everyone's gaze now veered to Dodo who kept her eyes trained on the inspector.

"While each of you sat in horrified shock, Lady Dorothea had the presence of mind to check the body and caught the scent of bitter almonds. Coupled with the deceased clutching her throat and her heightened color, it left no doubt in Lady Dorothea's mind that Adelaide Danforth had been poisoned by cyanide.

"She contacted the police almost immediately, telling them of her suspicions, which I confirmed.

"Who would kill a ninety-five-year-old woman? Our focus settled on the contents of her will." He clicked his heels together and began pacing in front of the flames. Dodo hoped the exaggerated theatrics would lull the murderer into a false sense of security.

"Several witnesses had heard the deceased talk about changing her will in her sleep the night before her death, and upon further investigation it became evident that Adelaide Danforth often threatened this action. It also became apparent that the family in the house knew she rarely followed through with her threats, or merely altered minor bequests. Outsiders, on the other hand, would probably not know this. Here was a motive I could sink my teeth into."

He gestured with his hand.

"This line of reasoning gained traction when it was discovered that Adelaide had a ruthless habit of promising wealth to manipulate people into doing her bidding," continued the inspector as he paced. "One after another, the people in the house told me that Adelaide had secretly promised that they would be named as the major beneficiary of her large fortune. None of these parties was aware of the others."

Dodo was watching Ruby and Lawrence as the inspector spoke. Their shoulders slumping more and more, reminding her of petulant children.

"Together with Lady Dorothea, I drew the conclusion that one of those promised the money must have heard the rumor about the threat to change the will and acted before that could take place, thus ensuring that their own legacy remained in force."

Ruby uncurled and her expression became defiant. "I would never!" she cried. "If you think for one moment—"

The inspector raised a finger. "I merely said that was the way our thoughts went at the beginning of the investigation."

Ruby stuck out her chin and crossed her arms over a matronly chest. "Oh."

"But the truth was that almost every guest in the house that night had been lied to by Adelaide," the inspector continued. "And when the will was read and it became apparent that she had not changed the contents, had never really changed the nucleus of it according to her solicitor, and by all accounts, had never intended to, I drew the misguided verdict that Adelaide had been murdered in vain."

He stopped pacing and placed a hand on the huge beam of wood that ran across the top of the fireplace. "Now we had a disappointed murderer who had not even benefited from their crime."

All he needs is a pipe to make the scene perfect.

"Lawrence Quintrell had been promised desperately needed funds. Before assisting Adelaide to attend an exclusive royal event to which she had not been invited, Lady Marlborough's son had also been flattered with the promise of a large endowment."

Lord Marlborough perked up when his name was mentioned.

"Even the vicar had been maneuvered into firing the choir director at Adelaide's request with the lure of much needed funds for the church roof." The inspector drew his brows in tight. "This made all three of you ideal suspects."

Reverend Valentine colored at this reference to his scheming.

"I say," spluttered Lord Marlborough, "I wasn't even here."

The inspector raised a hand to halt his lordship's defense.

"It seemed to be a classic case of greed."

The inspector turned dramatically, and Dodo had to hide a grin. "Then everything we thought we knew was turned upside down by the apparent suicide and confession of the maid, Warren." He paused until people began to shuffle in their seats.

He is rather good.

"Her death seemed like a straight up and down case of suicide brought on by guilt and briefly took the investigation in another direction. The sticking point was motive. What possible motive would a lady's maid with no apparent connection to Adelaide, have to kill her? We looked into her history to see if perhaps she too had been promised money by Adelaide, but our inquiries came up blank."

"You still haven't disclosed how you came to the conclusion that her death was *not* a suicide." said Mr. Danforth.

"Again, the credit must go to Lady Dorothea who questioned the authenticity of the note and encouraged me to compare it to another sample of Miss Warren's handwriting. Her maid, Lizzie, was able to get her hands on another piece of the dead maid's handwriting and though someone had gone to great pains to imitate Warren's hand, there were several small errors that proved the note to be a forgery."

Dodo looked round the room to see how *this* news was received. Everyone was staring at the inspector except Lady Marlborough who appeared to have fallen asleep.

"Now we knew the maid had been murdered. Why would the murderer need to silence her? Had Warren witnessed the murderer take the cyanide? Had she seen or heard something that, at the time did not mean much but after the murder, took on a whole new meaning? Did Warren threaten to expose the killer?"

He wagged his finger. "We could not know, but her murder sent us back to our original motive. The old lady's money."

Lawrence shifted in his chair catching the inspector's attention.

"After further investigation, we knew that Mr. Lawrence Quintrell had high hopes of his mother-in-law's will, having been assured that she sympathized with his financial plight and had vowed to make things right. With huge debts and other obligations," the inspector eyed Lawrence who squirmed, "dragging him down, could anyone blame him for helping Adelaide along to the next life a little more quickly?"

"Other obligations?" said his wife, Ruby sharply.

A telltale flash of color by his collar betrayed Lawrence's anxiety. "You know, the children," he lied.

Ruby frowned and her lips bunched up in a most unbecoming manner.

"Mrs. Quintrell was equally desperate to tip funds into the great hole of their finances."

Ruby's eyes flashed. "But I tell you, I would never! The very suggestion that I would kill my own mother. What do you think I am? An animal?" She was working herself up into a fury of righteous indignation.

"Unfortunately, declarations of innocence are not enough in my business, Mrs. Quintrell. Facts are what matters."

Ruby snorted.

The inspector pivoted. "As is often the case when we start investigating people's backgrounds, several important events were uncovered that I thought might have some bearing on the murders. Mrs. Danforth came under suspicion when we learned that her brother, Oliver, had drowned, here at *Knightsbrooke Priory*, in the lake. The case against her gained steam when archived newspaper articles revealed that the other occupant of the boat was none other than... Adelaide Danforth's husband, Rupert Danforth I. Perhaps she blamed him for not doing enough to save Oliver and after all these years exacted her revenge."

"Mummy?" said Beatrice.

"It's true," Etta stuttered. "And I did struggle with the fact for years, but I got over it long ago. My nervous disposition was

139

provoked by these murders, I admit, and I experienced a little mental crisis." She turned to the inspector. "But it was not a manifestation of guilt, Inspector. I am not a murderer."

The inspector merely nodded, and Rupert's father took his wife's hand in his.

Inspector Allingham repositioned his palm on the mantle. "These were the various puzzle pieces I was handed, and it took some time and collaboration to spread them out and make some sense of them. Frankly we had too many pieces and not enough knowledge of what the finished picture should look like.

"But the facts we had were that the poison was cyanide and it had come from a tin of rat killer in the kitchen. We even had a witness discover some of said crystals on the floor of the butler's pantry."

Lady Marlborough opened one eye to survey the room then clamped it shut.

"With Lady Dorothea's help I considered the impact a visit to the kitchen would have made if any of the guests had been to the larder during the day. We agreed that it would not have gone unnoticed. The obvious conclusion was that Warren had been approached to pilfer the poison since her presence would not have raised eyebrows. And then we caught a break."

He spun around again, and Dodo fought the urge to laugh. "One of the maids was besieged by guilt that she might have witnessed something important and came to see me. She had seen Warren exiting the pantry holding the tin of poison."

There were several gasps.

"Now I had evidence linking Warren to the actual murder."

Lady Marlborough muttered.

"But had she murdered Adelaide Danforth for a personal reason not yet discovered or...did she get the poison for someone else?"

He placed an elbow on the mantle. "I started to make a list of all the guests and who was most likely to ask the maid for help when Lady Dorothea, a savvy investigator, had me look at the case from an entirely different angle, suggesting that the motive for the crime dated much farther back."

Everyone moved forward in their seats.

140

"Lady Dorothea told me that Beatrice was reminiscing about her grandmother when she mentioned that she had chatted with her before she died. Adelaide had told Beatrice a story she had never heard before, that she had attended a ball before her marriage against her parents' wishes because she had come down with a contagious sickness. She had anticipated this particular ball for a long time and was eager to meet up with her beau. Determined to attend, and not feeling sick, she applied copious amounts of face powder to hide the rash and descended to the ball without her parent's knowledge."

A small hubbub erupted in the room.

The inspector raised his hand. "If you will indulge me a little longer," he begged. "At that ball, Adelaide danced with one Cedric Longthorpe, twin brother to Lady Marlborough. They danced only one set and then Adelaide danced with her beau, and it was all forgotten. But a few days later Cedric contracted scarlet fever. His was not a mild case and the disease damaged his heart so that a few years later, when struck by another common ailment, he died of a heart attack."

All eyes in the room were now fixed on Lady Marlborough who continued to pretend to be asleep.

"How could an unsteady, elderly person, who can only walk with a stick and has trouble with the stairs, have pulled off two murders? I had already concluded that Lady Marlborough was the most likely person to have the authority to persuade her maid to get the poison.

"I suggest that while you were all at the church for the Christmas Eve service, Adelaide recounted the long-forgotten story of the ball and the scarlet fever that she had recently told her granddaughter, to her old friend, and laughed about it. The story was brand new to Lady Marlborough and as her friend chuckled, she pieced together the incident with the illness and subsequent death of her beloved twin. Never had Lady Marlborough suspected that her darling twin brother had been killed by the selfish desires of a young woman over seventy years before. Incensed, she immediately hatched a plan to exact her revenge."

No one was looking at the inspector anymore, spellbound by the pile of sleeping woman in the chair. Dodo was gratified to see horror dawning on her son's features.

"But Lady Marlborough had a problem. She probably knew that poison was kept in the pantry from her youth, and if it was no longer there would gamble on finding some in the garden shed. But how would she physically get it? I put it to you that she called her maid to get it for her under some pretense—that she had seen a mouse in her room or some such. She guessed that no one would pay attention to a maid going into the pantry, that it would raise no questions. And besides, the kitchen staff were more than occupied preparing the Christmas Eve dinner.

"Warren took the crystals to her mistress with no qualms that her mistress was contemplating murder. Lady Marlborough was counting on Adelaide's death being put down to natural causes, and then Warren would have been none the wiser. But Lady Marlborough did not count on the detective skills of Lady Dorothea."

Dodo bowed her head.

"But when Adelaide Danforth's death was ruled a poisoning, Warren put two and two together and confronted her mistress. I imagine she either felt terrible guilt at having provided the means for her mistress to carry out the murder or she asked for money to keep her quiet.

She had to be stopped.

It would be easy to introduce the cyanide crystals into the maid's tea and silence her forever."

Lady Marlborough's eyes were still tightly shut but a small spasm in her jaw revealed that she was listening.

"Not having planned this second murder, Lady Marlborough made a mistake. She set about forging a suicide note."

"Monstrous accusations!" bellowed Lord Marlborough, moving away from his mother in horror. "Tell the inspector he is wrong, Mother!"

With great effort the old lady pried her eyes open, thrusting her lips out. "Why? Lady Dorothea has pretty much hit the nail on the head."

142

She heaved a sigh. "All these years I have mourned for my twin brother. To find that he need never have died so young, and the blame lay at the feet of my arrogant, indulged best friend, well, it was too much. Adelaide had lived a long and happy life and denied that to my brother by her selfish act. It was justice in my mind." She narrowed her gaze at the inspector. "But from where I am sitting this is all conjecture. Where is your solid evidence, the facts you spoke of? I shall deny everything I have said here today, in court."

With perfect timing the inspector withdrew a paper from his jacket pocket.

"As I mentioned, you made a mistake, Lady Marlborough. You wrote your son's telephone number on a sheet of paper from the pad where you practiced forging your maid's handwriting. You gave this paper to Lady Dorothea who today, rubbed the indentations with a pencil, revealing the words you had written before."

Lady Marlborough's eyes flared open. "No one will find an old lady like me guilty. They will consider my age and see that I was justified."

Lord Marlborough sat with his mouth open, staring in disbelief at the woman who had given birth to him.

"We shall see," declared the inspector.

He moved to the door and opened it to reveal two constables waiting for his sign, who came in to take Lady Marlborough away. One of them held up handcuffs.

"Is that really necessary?" asked her son in a desperate tone.

"Your mother has killed two people in cold blood. I think it highly appropriate," said Dodo, breaking her silence.

The officers shuffled the great lady out of the room and the occupants exploded with exclamations.

"You clever old thing!" whispered Rupert into Dodo's ear.

"When Beatrice told us the tale about the ball, I remembered who the other person was who spoke about scarlet fever. Then it was quite easy," she said. "And finding the evidence still in my waste basket was the icing on the cake."

Rupert's mother strode over to Dodo, hands outstretched, her face free of recrimination. "How can I ever thank you?" she said.

"I have treated you abysmally the last few days, blaming you for bringing a curse on the house. I see now how misguided I was. Can you ever forgive me?"

"Of course!" exclaimed Dodo winking at Rupert over his mother's shoulder.

Chapter 19

The fire was crackling, the scent of fir filling the air, and the low lights were shining on the red berries of the holly on the mantle. Dodo's feet were entwined with Rupert's as they cuddled on the maroon sofa.

The remnants of the Christmas present packaging Dodo had brought for Rupert, lay at their feet and the conservative silver cufflinks representing a polo player on his horse, were resting in Rupert's hand.

Everyone else had gone to bed except Lady Marlborough who was on her way to the police station with her son.

"Tell me again when you first suspected it was Lady Marlborough?" he asked running a hand up and down her arm.

"I had considered her as the most likely to be able to ask Warren to get the poison ages ago, but Adelaide was her best friend so I couldn't see a motive. Add to that her lack of mobility and it seemed impossible. How would she have killed Warren and got rid of the tea, or whatever she had given it to her in. In her testimony I remembered she had said that she wandered around after the reading of the will, *but no one had seen her.* I suspect she went straight to her room and that Warren confronted her about her suspicions and Lady Marlborough killed her right away but waited to raise the alarm. She probably sat there practicing the suicide note while the maid lay at her feet, dead." She shuddered.

"But as soon as I heard that story about your grandmother, I knew that was the motive *not* the money. Lucky for me the maids were all in chaos with so much murder and everything, otherwise that piece of paper would have been in the fire or taken by the dustbin men."

He pulled her even closer and kissed the top of her head. Her eyes misted.

"This isn't quite the way I imagined Christmas playing out." He sighed.

"Really? I thought perhaps you arranged it all to make sure I didn't get bored," she chuckled.

"I think people might be right, you are a murder magnet."

Dodo huffed. "It does seem that way, doesn't it?"

He squeezed her tighter. "If you weren't here, the murder would have happened anyway, and Lady Marlborough would have got away with it. There is no way anyone would have called the police for a routine death from old age."

"You are just saying that to make me feel better."

"No, I'm saying it because it is the truth. Justice has been served."

She wiggled her toes against his. "After all this, are you ready to meet my family?"

"Right now?"

"Not right away. I have some catching up with my sister to do. I have neglected her awfully because of you, and seeing Julia's sadness over Beatrice and the vicar, I think I need to spend some quality time with Didi. Just us."

"I don't know if I can survive being separated," he admitted.

"Me neither, to be honest, but I must. She deserves it. Didi is seeing an old flame of mine and I want to know all the details. Every last one of them."

"An old flame?"

"Yes, lovely chap but never sparked my blood like you do." She giggled.

"So, when can I come?"

"I shall have to ask, but Mummy has a holiday in the Greek Isles planned on a yummy yacht. She gets awfully depressed after Christmas and New Year's is over and simply has to get some sun. How does that sound?"

"I shall get my sailing whites ready." He grinned that show-stopping smile.

"You sail too?"

"There is no end to my talents, darling."

As he spoke, he lifted his arm. She raised her eyes to see a tiny sprig of mistletoe and a smile tugged at her own lips.

"I believe someone mentioned an encore performance," he said, his voice husky.

She lifted her lips. "Do your worst, Rupie."

The End

I hope you enjoyed this cozy mystery, *Murder on Christmas Eve*, and love Dodo as much as I do.

Interested in a free prequel to this series? Go to https://dl.bookfunnel.com/997vvive24 to download *Mystery at the Derby*.

Book one in the series, *Murder at Farrington Hall* is available on Amazon. https://amzn.to/31WujyS

"Dodo is invited to a weekend party at Farrington Hall. She and her sister are plunged into sleuthing when a murder occurs. Can she solve the crime before Scotland Yard's finest?"

Book two of the series, *Murder is Fashionable* is available on Amazon. https://amzn.to/2HBshwT

"Stylish Dodo Dorchester is a well-known patron of fashion. Hired by the famous Renee Dubois to support her line of French designs, she travels between Paris and London frequently. Arriving for the showing of the Spring 1923 collection, Dodo is thrust into her role as an amateur detective when one of the fashion models is murdered. Working under the radar of the French DCJP Inspector Roget, she follows clues to solve the crime. Will the murderer prove to be the man she has fallen for?"

Book three of the series, *Murder at the Races* is available on Amazon. https://amzn.to/2QIdYKM

"It is royal race day at Ascot, 1923. Lady Dorothea Dorchester, Dodo, has been invited by her childhood friend, Charlie, to an exclusive party in a private box with the added incentive of meeting the King and Queen.
Charlie appears to be interested in something more than friendship when a murder interferes with his plans. The victim is one of the guests from the box and Dodo cannot resist poking around. When Chief Inspector Blood of Scotland Yard is assigned to the case, sparks fly between them again. The chief inspector and Dodo have worked together on a case before and he welcomes her assistance with the prickly upper-class suspects. But where does this leave poor Charlie?

Dodo eagerly works on solving the murder which may have its roots in the distant past. Can she find the killer before they strike again?"

Book four of the series, *Murder on the Moors* is available on Amazon. https://amzn.to/38SDX8d

When you just want to run away and nurse your broken heart but murder comes knocking.

"Lady Dorothea Dorchester, Dodo, flees to her cousins' estate in Dartmoor in search of peace and relaxation after her devastating break-up with Charlie and the awkward attraction to Chief Inspector Blood that caused it.
Horrified to learn that the arch-nemesis from her schooldays, Veronica Shufflebottom, has been invited, Dodo prepares for disappointment. However, all that pales when one of the guests disappears after a ramble on the foggy moors. Presumed dead, Dodo attempts to contact the local police to report the disappearance only to find that someone has tampered with the ancient phone. The infamous moor fog is too thick for safe travel and the guests are therefore stranded.
Can Dodo solve the case without the help of the police before the fog lifts?"

Book five of the series, *Murder in Limehouse* is available on Amazon.

https://amzn.to/3pw2wzQ

Aristocratic star she may be, but when her new love's sister is implicated in a murder, Dodo Dorchester rolls up her designer sleeves and plunges into the slums of London.

Dodo is back from the moors of Devon and diving into fashion business for the House of Dubois with one of the most celebrated department stores in England, while she waits for a call from Rupert Danforth, her newest love interest.
Curiously, the buyer she met with at the store, is murdered that night in the slums of Limehouse. It is only of passing interest

because Dodo has no real connection to the crime. Besides, pursuing the promising relationship that began in Devon is a much higher priority.

However, fate has a different plan. Rupert's sister, Beatrice, is arrested for the murder of the very woman Dodo conducted business with at the fashionable store. Now she must solve the crime to protect the man she is fast falling in love with.

Can she do it before Beatrice is sent to trial?

For more information about the series go to my website at www.annsuttonauthor.com and subscribe to my newsletter.

You can also follow me on Facebook at: https://www.facebook.com/annsuttonauthor

About the Author

Agatha Christie plunged me into the fabulous world of reading when I was 10. I was never the same. I read every one of her books I could lay my hands on. Mysteries remain my favorite genre to this day - so it was only natural that I would eventually write my own.

Born and raised in England, writing fiction about my homeland keeps me connected.

After finishing my degree in French and Education and raising my family, writing has become a favorite hobby.

I hope that Dame Agatha would enjoy Dodo Dorchester at much as I do.

Acknowledgements

My proof-reader – Tami Stewart

The mother of a large and growing family who reads like the wind with an eagle eye. Thank you for finding little errors that have been missed.

My editor – Jolene Perry of Waypoint Author Academy

Sending my work to editors is the most terrifying part of the process for me but Jolene offers correction and constructive criticism without crushing my fragile ego.

My cheerleader, marketer and IT guy – Todd Matern

A lot of the time during the marketing side of being an author I am running around with my hair on fire. Todd is the yin to my yang. He calms me down and takes over when I am yelling at the computer.

My beta readers – Francesca Matern, Stina Van Cott,

Your reactions to my characters and plot are invaluable.

My critique group – Mary Thomas, Laurie Turner, Lisa McKendrick

For reading my stuff and your helpful suggestions

The Writing Gals and 20Booksto50k for their FB author community and their YouTube tutorials

These sites give so much of their time to teaching their Indie author followers how to succeed in this brave new publishing world. Thank you.